THE DEVIL'S

Nick Ryan

A World War 3 Technothriller Action Event

Copyright © 2024 Nicholas Ryan

The right of Nicholas Ryan to be identified as the author of this work has been asserted by him in accordance with the copyright, Designs and Patents Act 1988.

This is a work of fiction. Names, characters, places, and incidents either are the product of the author's imagination or are used fictitiously. Any resemblance to actual persons, living or dead, events, or locales is entirely coincidental.

All rights reserved. No part of this publication may be reproduced, stored in or introduced into a retrieval system, or transmitted, in any form, or by any other means (electronic, mechanical, photocopying, recording or otherwise) without the prior written permission of the author. Any person who does any unauthorized act in relation to this publication may be liable to criminal prosecution and civil claims for damages.

Dedication:
As always, this book is dedicated to my fiancé, Ebony.
'Ain't no sunshine when she's gone...'

About the Series:

The WW3 novels are a chillingly authentic collection of action-packed combat thrillers that envision a modern war where the world's superpowers battle on land, air and sea using today's military hardware.

Each title is a 50,000-word stand-alone adventure that forms part of an ever-expanding series.

Website: https://www.worldwar3timeline.com

Links to other titles in the collection:
- Charge to Battle
- Enemy in Sight
- Viper Mission
- Fort Suicide
- The Killing Ground
- Search and Destroy
- Airborne Assault
- Defiant to the Death
- A Time for Heroes
- Oath of Honor
- The Devil's Detail

NEWS ALERT:

Nick Ryan is now creating short World War III combat movies!

Check out the 'Nick Ryan's WW3 Films' Patreon page for more information about the military action movie currently in production.

patreon.com/NickRyanWW3Films

The Fight for Germany

For the first few weeks following the outbreak of war in Europe, the Russian military swept all before them, capturing the Baltic States with ease and then surging west through Poland; a mighty juggernaut of artillery, tanks and men, driving relentlessly towards Berlin.

The NATO allies were surprised by the violence and the venom of the Russian advance. They were pushed back; forced to fight in small numbers against an avalanche of enemy armor.

But by the time the Russians reached the German border, the allies had managed to mobilize and coordinate their units into a cohesive fighting force. Allied fighter jets took a dreadful toll on the enemy vanguard. Russia's great military machine began to shudder to a halt, so by the time the two massed armies faced each other across the Oder River, both sides had become ground down by exhaustion.

On the surface, Russia's early advances westwards were a spectacular success, and the Russian media was quick to lionize their generals and the brave fighting men who were at war for the Motherland. But beneath the glossy, glowing veneer of triumphant headlines, the truth behind Russia's land gains was far more disturbing.

Every inch of ground the Russians had won had come at a terrible cost of both men and precious military equipment. Their ranks of front-line elite combat troops were quickly thinned and replaced with B-Army units shunted west on trains like cattle. The regiments of modern tanks that made up the spearhead of the army had been decimated by allied attrition, and the air-wings of latest generation Russian fighters were falling from the sky at a rate three times higher than allied losses.

Inevitably, the degradation in troop quality and armor began to slow the Russian army's progress to a ponderous trundle. The lightning-swift assaults that had typified the first days of the war were replaced by dour pitched battles, and the death toll rose steadily until not even the Russian media could blithely camouflage the losses.

In Moscow, small groups of citizens who began to protest against the war were quickly arrested by Russian security forces. Voices raised in objection were brutally silenced. But the slow fuse had been lit, and the Russian President recognized that his country was on the brink of becoming a tinderbox of rebellious discontent.

The only things the proud Russian peasant people responded to was the nostalgia of past patriotic glory and military triumph. The President knew his people. He realized in order to quell the rising restlessness amongst the masses, he must give them one more savage, crushing victory.

Determined to maintain the momentum of his army's advance, and keen to suppress the growing rumbles of political dissent, the Russian President summonsed his western front generals to the Kremlin and delivered a chilling ultimatum, acutely aware that the Motherland would either rise, or be crushed to ashes, as a consequence of his decision.

Berlin had to be seized, and seized fast.
Or else the war would be lost.

RUSSIAN FORWARD COMMAND POST
TWO MILES EAST OF GORZYCA,
POLAND-GERMANY BORDER

Prologue:

When Chief of the General Staff Army General Mikhail Timoshyn's Mil Mi-17 helicopter finally touched down on the outskirts of bomb-ravaged Gorzyca, the Russian CINC-West gave a great sigh, then sat back and stared vacantly into space. He felt sick with worry, his weary mind picking over his instructions from the Kremlin and the inevitable bloody consequences of the orders he had received.

There was no official welcome party to greet him on his return to the western front because any gathering of pomp and ceremony so close to the fighting might attract NATO jets, so he was met by a single driver standing beside a lone mud-spattered UAZ light vehicle. The driver saluted crisply, quivering at attention, pale-faced with terror. Timoshyn glared at the young soldier with baleful eyes and then bundled himself, grumbling and muttering darkly, into the vehicle.

He was impossibly tired and the long return flight from Moscow had only deepened his despair. From the passenger seat, he peered out at the shell-cratered wasteland of Poland while the little UAZ jounced and bucked over the rutted ruins of road.

The sky was sullen and grey with storm clouds, and the air reverberated with the relentless thunder of Russian artillery pounding the allied positions across the border. The stench of death hung like a sweet-sickly pall over the misery of the battlefront, cloying and rancid in the General's nostrils. Destroyed Russian T-90 tanks lined the edge of the ruined road and rotting, bloated corpses lay clumped together in clusters. Crows were picking at the remains, and rats scurried in the shadows.

Timoshyn reached the forward command post and climbed heavily from the UAZ. His boots made obscene little sucking sounds in the muddy quagmire. He pulled his heavy coat close around his slumped shoulders and ducked beneath the bunker's sandbagged lintel, then stood for a long moment, his eyes adjusting to the cavern-like gloom. The underground shelter stank of unwashed bodies and the air was hazed blue by cheap cigarette smoke. He sensed the fraught tension in the air immediately as heads turned in his direction.

"Everybody out now," Timoshyn growled. "Only Lieutenant-General Stavatesky will remain."

There were twenty pale-faced staff officers in the bunker, gathered around map-littered trestle tables. For a moment they looked astonished, and then, like chastened schoolchildren, they filed past Timoshyn, out into the dull afternoon light, leaving the Chief of the General Staff alone with his deputy.

Lieutenant-General Oleg Stavatesky was fifty-seven years old; a relatively young man for such a position of military power. A graduate of the Frunze Military Academy, he had served with distinction commanding the 42nd Guards Motor Rifle Division, rising up through the Russian military hierarchy over a number of years to finally command the Leningrad Military District before being appointed deputy chief of the General Staff. He was considered one of the Russian Army's brightest and cruellest military minds – a ruthless man, nicknamed the 'Terror of Tajikistan', he was bald-headed and built like a bare-knuckle fighter.

"Welcome back, my General," Stavatesky inclined his head, then looked Timoshyn discretely up and down, careful to keep his face a mask. The General's face was pallid and his eyes deep-set within folds of rumpled flesh, underscored by the dark bruises of exhaustion. "I trust your meeting with the President and the Defense Minister went well?"

"It did not," Timoshyn fished a cigarette from his pocket and lit it. He inhaled deeply and peered through the cloud of blue smoke. "It was a fucking disaster if you must know."

Stavatesky looked genuinely astonished. His face crumpled into an expression of uncomprehending dismay. "But we have achieved so much! In barely six weeks we have seized the Baltic States and conquered Poland. Now we are at the border with

Germany and the allies are reeling to recover their positions. What more could the Kremlin expect of us?"

General Timoshyn growled like a bear. "Our political masters are fools," he snarled, then fought visibly to regain his temper before going on. "The President and the Minister for Defense know nothing about modern warfare, nor logistics. They demand we drive immediately towards Berlin. We have no time to secure our position and no time to bring more men and equipment forward – even if they were available. The President wants the allies crushed quickly – and he has given us just two weeks to make this miracle happen."

"Two weeks? But that is impossible," Stavatesky balked. "The allies command the skies. As soon as we move, their fighters swarm across the border and pound our columns to pieces."

It was a cruel truth of the war so far. Before hostilities had begun, the Russian generals in the field had been assured by Moscow that Russian air power would dominate the skies over the battlefield. That had not happened. America's fifth-generation fighters had proved far superior to their Russian counterparts.

"I said the same," General Timoshyn seemed suddenly to sag with exhaustion. His expression turned bereft with despair. "I told the President that such an attack was impossible without more men and more tanks."

"So, we will be reinforced?"

"No – and do you know why, comrade deputy? I'll tell you why," the General's voice rose again in sudden exasperation. "Because the Motherland has no more tanks to give us!"

Stavatesky shook his head and frowned. "Comrade General, I do not understand."

"It is simple," the General said. "Our great victories have come at a cost of men and armor, yes?"

Stavatesky inclined his head. It was not politic to talk about losses. The Russian media, under tight control from Moscow, had been careful to downplay the extent of casualties resulting from the fighting so that only those in the upper echelons of the

Russian government knew the staggering true cost of each triumph. Privately, both men knew how bloody the fighting across Poland and the Balkans had been. The allies, despite conceding ground, had been relentlessly bleeding the Russian war machine dry.

"We have had some losses," the deputy CINC-West admitted carefully.

Timoshyn scoffed, then his voice turned sober and serious. "Oleg, only in front of the army must we play the role of hard-nosed commanders. In here, it is just you and me. We are both old warriors. We know the truth of the matter. Our tanks have proved inferior to the tanks of the western allies, and our men are not of the same caliber as those heroes who seized Berlin in 1945. Our middle-ranking officers are poorly trained and most of our men currently fighting on the frontlines were fucking farmhands and factory workers just six months ago."

"But if we had more tanks..."

"And if we could find a way to overcome the allied anti-tank missiles," General Timoshyn added. "Those fucking things have crippled us. They've turned our best regiments into scrap metal."

"We need more T-90s."

"Well, there are no more T-90s available to us, nor even T-72s. Our factories cannot build the fighting machines we need quickly enough to resupply our front lines because our losses to this point of the war have been so heavy. So instead, the Minister for Defense has given orders to re-activate several Siberian factories to refurbish our stores of fucking T-62s!"

"No!" Stavatesky's face paled. He looked like he might be sick.

"It is true!" General Timoshyn growled and his voice rose in exasperation. "I heard it directly from the Minister. The Kremlin plans on reinforcing our invasion army with sixty-year-old light tanks that haven't seen action since before the Cold fucking War. And with these antiques we are expected to push the allies back towards France and seize Berlin! Within the next fourteen days."

"It cannot be done, my General," Stavatesky conceded.

"It must be," Timoshyn crushed his cigarette beneath the heel of his boot. "You know what happened to the last CINC-West and his Deputy who failed..."

It was a sinister moment of foreboding, fraught with heavy significance. The Russian government had never been forgiving of military failure. Most commanders were led away in disgrace, never to be heard of again. More than a few had been backed up against a wall and summarily shot in the aftermath of a fiasco.

Stavatesky paled noticeably. He had political aspirations. His glittering military career was just the first step in the carefully-laid plans of an ambitious man. Now, quite suddenly, all his years of stellar achievement were at risk.

For a long moment, neither man spoke and there was only the distant incessant sound of far-away artillery fire.

"Stavatesky," General Timoshyn began quietly, "I have been a good and loyal servant of the Motherland for all my life. I have fought our wars, and I have killed to defend our country. I have sent both my sons to war, and I have suffered the deprivations of a soldier without question. But we are our own worst enemy. Our tactics have changed little since 1917. We have become predictable. The allies know our every move because they have been studying us at war for a century. They know every attack is announced by an artillery barrage and preceded by an air attack. They know how we use our tanks and infantry in combination. We have been ruled by doctrine instead of imagination. We have relied too much on brute force and not enough on innovation. Our highest-ranking officers are not the best and the brightest – they are the most docile and dutiful to the government. The result is a fighting force that has only one way to fight a war. It will be the ruin of us."

General Timoshyn stopped suddenly, aware of the risk he had taken. Such unpatriotic assessments could easily be construed as treasonable, even if this was a private conversation. Stavatesky smiled benignly for a moment to reassure his general that his protests would remain their secret, and then his eyes turned glittering with a spark of inspiration.

"You are right, my General," the deputy CINC-West conceded, barely whispering the words. "But... maybe..."

"But maybe what?" Timoshyn pushed.

"Perhaps our predictability can be used as its own weapon," suddenly Stavatesky was alive with energy, his mind sharp as a razor. Fatigue and despondency sloughed from him in an instant as he lunged for a map on a nearby table. He spread the chart out and peered hard at the terrain, his hawk-like eyes searching, his nimble mind scheming.

General Timoshyn joined his deputy at the table, peering over the other man's shoulder. The map showed the western front stretching from Guben in the south, all the way north to Schwedt. The chart was a chaos of lines and notations showing troop dispositions, artillery parks, munitions dumps, fuel storage dumps and a second echelon of B-grade reserve units that were being rushed west from Warsaw.

"Here is the state of the war," Deputy Stavatesky splayed his fingers and swept his hand over the map. "Later today many of our remaining T-90s and T-72s will lead an attack on the twin towns of Bad Freienwalde and Wriezen, ten miles across the German border. Our air strikes are timed to commence at thirteen hundred hours and the artillery will begin its bombardment on the allied positions in another hour or so."

Timoshyn grunted. All this information he already knew. He had authorized the attack before being recalled to Moscow.

"So?"

"So, our attack will most likely fail," Stavatesky said bluntly. "Once the allies know we are coming they will reinforce their position, or concede the towns to us temporarily before launching a counter-attack."

"So?"

"So, we must delay this attack for twenty-four hours and then use the predictability of our advance to conceal something else – something unexpected."

General Timoshyn straightened with a weary sigh. "I have no time, nor the patience for games, comrade. Speak plainly."

Stavatesky inclined his head in concession. "General, forgive me. But I have an idea."

"An idea?" the general looked astonished.

"A surprise attack against the allies."

"Where?"

"Here," Stavatesky stabbed his finger at the map, pointing to a small town across the German border, several miles south of Guben.

Timoshyn frowned, bewildered, and looked closely at the map. "Klein Gastrose?" he read the name of the hamlet. "It's a pointless shithole on the arse-end of the war, several miles south of the frontlines," he said. "We have no troops there, no tanks, no artillery."

"Exactly!" Deputy Stavatesky straightened, his face tight, his features working with excitement. "If we no longer have the tanks we need to bludgeon our way through the allied lines, then we must find a new way to fight. Instead of the hammer against the anvil, we must become like water. We must flow around the enemy and erode their strength from behind."

"Behind?"

"Look again at the map, my General. The intersection that little hamlet is built around runs north towards Berlin, behind and parallel to the allied troop positions. If we can seize the intersection, we can threaten the entire enemy position."

"But how can we pivot our whole army quickly enough to catch the allies off guard, Stavatesky? Their satellites, their reconnaissance planes, their drones. They will spot any major troop movement and counter within hours."

"Not if we behave in a manner completely contrary to what the allies expect," the deputy waggled his finger like a schoolteacher addressing an addled child. "We mount an attack with infantry alone; two or three battalions in BMPs. No artillery support. No fighter cover; nothing to announce our advance. Then, once we seize the intersection, we can pour our best remaining tanks and a regiment of mechanized infantry into the countryside behind the allied lines. The entire western front might collapse."

"Two battalions of infantry in BMPs?" General Timoshyn blinked owlishly as the intriguing innovation of the idea became clear to him.

"Yes. Any force greater would attract allied attention, as you so rightly noted. It would be a surprise attack from a predictable enemy. The allies will not suspect anything until it is too late to recognize the peril we have placed them in."

General Timoshyn considered the plan carefully for several minutes. It went against everything he ever understood about warfare. It was so contrary to accepted Russian military doctrine it seemed almost obscene.

On an impulse, and still undecided, he bellowed for the bunker's senior staff to return. As they filed back into the dim shelter, he drew one of his officers aside.

"When are our next attacks going in?" he demanded, looming over the man.

The officer faltered for a moment. "The next probing attack against the enemy is scheduled for one hour from now," the staff officer checked his watch. He could feel himself breaking out into an anxious sweat. The General's presence was intimidating, and the man licked his lips nervously.

"Where?"

"A town called Urad, my General."

"Show me!" Timoshyn demanded.

A series of small assaults had been planned in the hours leading up to the Russian army's intended drive towards Bad Freienwalde and Wriezen – designed to stretch the enemy's defenses, and to cause confusion before the main assault.

The staff officer led Timoshyn and Stavatesky to a map of the Polish border and pointed.

"It is a bridging assault across the Oder River at Urad," the site was marked on the map. The Polish border town of Urad stood about eleven kilometers to the north west of Cybinka.

Timoshyn leaned over the map thoughtfully. On the opposite side of the river from the Polish settlement was a small

German hamlet named Aurith, isolated from the nearest neighboring German towns by a five-kilometer-wide ribbon of farm fields and plowed ground. Lying beside the map Timoshyn found a couple of grainy satellite photos that showed a close-up stretch of the Oder River. An old broken bridge was highlighted, and along both banks on either side of the river appeared the remnants of a dozen or more old stone causeways, thrusting out from both embankments like fingers stretching towards each other. Timoshyn guessed that at some time in the past, this shallow, narrow section of the Oder had been spanned in at least a dozen places.

It was the ideal location for a river crossing or a bridging assault.

He made up his mind.

"Deputy Stavatesky, fetch your heavy jacket. We are going to witness this bridging assault personally. After the attack goes in, I will make my decision about your plan."

*

The General's vehicle arrived on the outskirts of Urad just as the Russian artillery began its bombardment across the river, first pounding a string of German villages further inland and then concentrating their fire on the outskirts of Aurith. The tiny hamlet was defended by two companies of Belgian light infantry from the 12/13th Prince Leopold Battalion of the Line, with the remaining two companies of the unit entrenched on the flanks.

Timoshyn and Stavatesky were driven to an elevated rise of ground east of Urad from where they could observe the attack.

The afternoon was bleak and cold. A chill nagging wind from the north had pushed a layer of thick rainclouds over the German frontier so the world was grey and brooding as the Russian artillery began its grim work.

The Russian CINC-West and his Deputy were escorted to a BTR-80 parked amongst a grove of trees where the Major-

General in charge of the assault was in urgent conversation with his support staff.

The senior officer blinked in astonishment when he saw Timoshyn approaching and snapped a hasty salute.

"My General!" he blustered, suddenly ashen-faced with alarm and dread. "I was not told you had already returned from your meetings in Moscow."

Timoshyn swatted away the senior officer's garble with an irritated swish of his hand.

"Relax," he said wearily. "General Stavatesky and I are simply here to observe. Go about your work, man."

The Major-General winced, then nodded. Timoshyn and Stavatesky turned and took a long moment to survey the battlefield with binoculars. At the foot of the rise they stood atop stretched the small town of Urad. Some of the buildings had suffered bomb damage, but others remained intact. Timoshyn panned his binoculars west until the broken bridge and several old stone causeways across the Oder came into view. On the banks of the river, hidden from allied view behind a fringing palisade of trees, were piles of bridging equipment and engineering vehicles.

The two commanders surveyed the ground for a moment and then turned their attention to the hamlet beyond the far bank of the river. They could see the great scar of earthworks north and south of the settlement that marked the position of the enemy trenches, and they could see, too, that the village itself had been heavily sandbagged and fortified. As they watched on, another barrage of Russian artillery shells hit the hamlet, flattening houses and sending great clouds of smoke and dust into the air.

Timoshyn set down his binoculars and beckoned the Major-General to him.

"Tell me the plan," he demanded gruffly.

The Major-General glanced at his watch, then turned his eyes skyward. "Two SU-25s are inbound as we speak, my General. Once the artillery finishes its fire mission, the *grachs* will straf the buildings in the village and the enemy trenches. Then the artillery has orders to fire smoke."

"And under the veil of smoke, the bridging assault across the river will commence?" Stavatesky assumed.

"Yes, sir."

The Deputy CINC-West nodded. It was a textbook operation, straight out of some antique Russian military manual from the 1950s.

The engineers were troops from the 16th Regiment – part of the 20th Guards Combined Arms Army which had fought in Latvia, and the men who would lead the assault were veterans from the 84th Reconnaissance Battalion, supported by a brigade of the 252nd Motor Rifle Regiment, all mounted in amphibious BTR-80 armored personnel carriers. The APCs were parked two miles to the east of the town, concealed in a patch of woodland with the assault troops who were waiting for the orders to mount their vehicles and advance.

The Russian artillery continued to pound the Belgian positions across the river for two more minutes and then stopped abruptly, leaving a dense cloud of drifting black smoke and burning building rubble in their wake. Then the two Frogfoots came screaming in from the northeast, scraping the treetops as they flashed past.

The Su-25 had been a mainstay of the Russian Air Force for around forty years. The subsonic single-seat jet was designed to provide close support for Russian ground forces. Heavily armored, it was a smaller, lighter and faster counterpart to the American A-10 Warthog.

The two Frogfoots flashed across the Oder barely one hundred feet above the ground and began strafing the village of Aurith, their 30mm AO-17A twin-barrel guns installed in the underside of the fuselage roaring death. They swept past their target in just a few savage seconds, then climbed and banked sharply to the northwest, turning to make a return run, their wing pylons bristling with air-to-ground missiles and cluster bombs.

Then suddenly two German Luftwaffe Eurofighter Typhoons appeared through the cloud cover further to the west. The twin-engined supersonic multirole fighters were part of the *Taktisches Luftwaffengeschwader* 71 'Richthofen' fighter wing, based out of Wittmundhafen Air Base, northwest of Bremen before the war but now operating closer to the Polish border flying combat air patrols.

The sleek Typhoons were vectored to their targets by German Tactical Air Command in Schönewalde and, using their speed advantage, closed quickly on the unsuspecting Su-25s.

The first Frogfoot disappeared in a flaming fireball five kilometers west of Aurith and fell to the ground in a shower of twisted, burning debris. The second Russian Su-25 lasted just two seconds longer, struck by an air-to-air AMRAAM as it leveled in flight and began to flee in panic back towards the Polish border.

"Yebat'!" Stavatesky had watched the two Russian ground attack jets shot from the sky through his binoculars and swore foully. He turned to the Major-General commanding the operation red-faced with temper. "Where are our fucking Su-34 fighter-bombers? Why are they not flying top cover?"

Since the outbreak of war, the Russians had made it a policy to operate the Su-25s and Su-34s in packs during combat operations with the Su-34s protecting the airspace above a ground attack so the Frogfoots could work with impunity. The tactic had worked well in the Baltics and in eastern Poland.

The Major-General shrugged his shoulders and looked pathetic with humiliation. "My General, I do not command the Motherland's air forces. They have suffered many losses in recent weeks. Perhaps..."

General Timoshyn turned and glared accusingly at both men. "That is a question for the aftermath," he cut their bickering off abruptly, "and I will be certain to get answers. But for now, Major-General, get on with your work. The enemy troops have been hammered by artillery and strafed by our jets.

Now send your men across and secure the far side of the river. Immediately."

As if stage directed and scripted, the Russian artillery began blanketing the far riverbank with a thick veil of white smoke that rose in a curtain between the village and the west bank of the Oder. For three long minutes the smoke continued to fall while the Major-General barked orders down the radio to the waiting column of armored personnel carriers.

The first men to cross the river were the 84th Reconnaissance Battalion in their BTR-80s. The amphibious APCs plunged headlong towards the riverbank with their trim vanes already erected and their tire pressure lowered. The water was just a few meters deep, and the river was narrow. The APCs waded through the silty murk, pushing small bow waves ahead of them and emerged on the western bank where they stopped suddenly and began firing through the smoke towards the German hamlet with their 14.5mm KPVT heavy machine guns. Once back on dry land, the recce troops bundled out of their vehicles and threw themselves down in cover, securing the far bank and establishing a bridgehead.

On cue, the Russian engineers, hidden in the fringe of forest near the east bank of the Oder, suddenly emerged from cover to begin the process of bridging the river. Working in teams, and urged to action by their growling officers, the engineers worked themselves into a lather of frenzied sweat and then six MTU-72 bridge laying vehicles broke through the fringe of trees. The MTU was derived from the T-72 main battle tank and carried a vast folding bridge span atop its hull. The six-ton single-span was twenty meters long and could be used in pairs to reach across watercourses up to a hundred feet wide.

The MTUs were awkward, ungainly abominations, mud-streaked and filthy with grime, belching great clouds of black smoke from their heaving engines as they pirouetted and jinked into position along the east bank of the river. It took just a few minutes for each vehicle to deploy its span of bridge. The MTUs backed away, their work done, and Timoshyn turned with his binoculars to search for the advancing armored column that would make the crossing. He saw them, already racing towards the river, swerving along the town's main street at speed.

The soldiers from the 252nd Motor Rifle Regiment were battle-worn veterans who had already fought gallantly in Lithuania. Hunched down in their troop transports they went about the grim process of preparing themselves for combat while the vehicles jounced and swayed towards the river.

"Well done," Timoshyn acknowledged the Major-General grudgingly. "Your attack has been well-coordinated, and the bridging operation completed with admirable efficiency."

"Thank you, my General," the senior officer blushed like a shy young girl given a compliment.

So far, the assault across the river had gone to plan, except for the intervention of the German Typhoons. With the first three perilous stages of the crossing completed, and not a single casualty reported by enemy fire, the fourth step, CINC-West knew, was to expand and secure the bridgehead line, which meant getting more men across the Oder in preparation to foil an allied counterattack.

He felt himself begin to relax. He turned and shot a glance at Stavatesky with a smug, satisfied smile on his face.

"Textbook predictability is acceptable, provided it is done in a manner that the enemy is powerless to challenge," CINC-West said archly.

"Perhaps," his Deputy inclined his head. "We shall soon see, General. The allies must challenge the crossing – unless they are leading us into a well-laid trap."

That comment made Timoshyn blink. He had attributed the success of the crossing to a well-performed operation, executed in the Russian manner. His Deputy's warning gave him a fluttering moment of uneasy trepidation. He clamped the binoculars back to his eyes and peered hard at the river, just as the first BTR-80 reached the east bank and mounted one of the three waiting bridges.

The line of APCs had split into smaller columns in order to make the crossing, minimizing the time it would take to get the troops and vehicles to the far riverbank. The vehicles in the vanguard slowed as they reached the waiting bridges and the line of trailing APCs was forced to compress, each driver impatient and feeling suddenly exposed.

"Go! Move quickly!" General Timoshyn heard himself mutter beneath his breath, railing against his own impatience as his anxiety steadily climbed. The Russians still only had a company of the 84th Reconnaissance Battalion and about a dozen BTRs on the far bank. Until those men could be reinforced, the position was still perilous. Every second counted.

The first of the BTR-80s began the slow traverse of the river, engines in low gear, and the seconds of suspenseful tension drew out until Timoshyn felt himself run cold with sweat.

"Hurry!" he growled, irritated with frustration. "Move faster you fools!"

The battle seemed suspended on a knife-edge.

And then disaster struck.

The four Fairchild Republic A-10C Thunderbolt IIs that suddenly appeared over the battlefield were from the 74th Fighter Squadron, based at Moody AFB, Georgia, but operating from a German airfield west of Berlin since the outbreak of war. They came in low over the surrounding urban landscape like avenging angels, responding to an urgent call from a JTAC (Joint Terminal Attack Controller) aboard an AWACS patrolling the air west of the border. The Belgian infantry defending the hamlet had sent out a desperate 'All Players' call for air support and the Warthogs were on the warpath.

"*Yebat'!*" General Stavatesky swore again when he saw the four dark specs drop out of the clouds, his shoulders slumping with bitter inevitability. He pointed to the incoming American fighters and General Timoshyn felt a gut-tripping sense of sudden despair. Following the outbreak of fighting across Europe, the Russians had quickly come to loathe and despise the fearsome A-10. "*Nositeli smerti,*" Stavatesky warned helplessly. "The bringers of death."

General Timoshyn saw the approaching enemy fighters and turned red-faced with blustering rage to the Major-General in command. "Where are your fucking SAM defenses, man?"

Two Pantsir-S1 launchers mounted on KamAZ-6560 8x8 trucks were parked a mile to the east, beyond the outskirts of Urad. Three seconds after the A-10s appeared on their tracking radars the on-board fire control system acquired the targets and unleashed four 57E6 two-stage missiles into the sky.

The missiles flashed low across the sky on long trails of grey smoke and the incoming A-10s immediately 'went cold', lowering their speed to reduce their heat signatures and dispensing chaff. The formation broke apart and began to bank across the sky, defending themselves against the looming threat with their sophisticated ECM suites fully activated.

The Russian missiles flashed past harmlessly and the Hog pilots steeled themselves to make their attack. In these situations, conventional combat tactics required the A-10s to suppress the Russian SAM threat before attacking the enemy's ground forces, but the immediate urgency of the moment rendered that approach impossible, despite the increased risk. It meant the pilots would need to run the gauntlet of surface-to-air missiles while simultaneously receiving ground fire.

The Hogs had responded to the 'All Players' call from the Belgian infantry fully loaded; their external pylon stations bristling with canisters of Mk 20 Rockeye cluster bombs, AGM-65D Maverick missiles, and two AIM-9 Sidewinder air-to-air missiles. The pilot in the lead A-10 ran his gaze quickly across the cockpit's two multifunction displays and then the up-front controller located below the HUD to scan his on-board systems. He nosed the Hog lower to the ground and launched a Maverick air-to-surface missile at the nearest Pantsir. With the missile inbound the pilot then lined the nose of his Hog up with the river, dropping level with the trees as he followed the meandering Oder closer to the crossing.

The Maverick missed its target and exploded in a grove of nearby woods. The Russian SAMs unleashed another flurry of missiles but by then the lead Hog was less than a kilometer from its prey.

The A-10's main armament was the 30mm GAU-8/A seven-barrel Avenger Gatling gun, capable of firing over four thousand rounds per minute. The Hog pilot saw the column of stalled Russian BTR-80s and smiled a cruel, mirthless smile. It was a target-rich environment; a slaughterhouse of stationary enemy armor.

Some of the stranded Russian troops on the riverbank saw the incoming threat and tried to abandon their transports. Some vehicle commanders screamed at their gunners to open fire on the inbound danger. A shudder of panic seemed to wash through the Russian column and a moment later that terror turned to devastation and despair.

The sound of the Warthog firing was like a hellish juddering jackhammer of wrath. The aircraft seemed to shake in the air and the nose disappeared in a billowing veil of smoke as the awesome power of the Gatling gun was unleashed. Three BTRs were destroyed in the first few seconds, ripped to pieces by the killing power of the gun. Men died inside their vehicles as they were torn into scrap metal.

The first Hog flashed past the river crossing, banking to the west and climbing after it finished its lethal swoop. The pilot dispensed chaff as a precaution then circled away to make room for the next A-10.

More panic fire from the ground rushed up to meet the incoming Warthog, thudding into the aircraft's armor protection. An unseen MANPAD flashed past the cockpit on a twisting trail of smoke, missing the jet by less than fifty meters. The pilot lined his sights onto a cluster of stalled enemy APCs still on the riverbank and unleashed hell.

Another handful of BTR-80s were either destroyed or disabled. One caught on fire and burned fiercely, incinerating the seven soldiers trapped inside the steel coffin. One of the APCs sank down on its suspension, its hull riddled with jagged bullet-holes and every tire shredded. More smoke poured into the sky, struck through with lurid flashes of fire. The sounds of the beleaguered Russian infantry rose to a wail of helpless horror.

The Pantsir systems fired again, unleashing another belated flurry of missiles at the Warthogs as they finished their attacking runs and began to flash away to the west, but they were defeated by chaff and ECM jamming.

General Timoshyn turned away from the horror, grey faced, and his features crumpled with the humiliating sting of defeat. He didn't need to watch the last two Warthogs savage the remnants of the armored column; he heard the explosions and the screams. He set down his binoculars and for a moment it looked like CINC-West might weep with frustration.

The Major-General commanding the assault looked appalled; almost disbelieving. In just seventy-five savage seconds his entire operation had been torn to shreds; triumph snatched away from him. He stared aghast at the Armageddon-like scene strewn across the riverbank with a look of utter impotent dismay.

General Timoshyn lit a cigarette. His hands were shaking. The American A-10s had turned the riverbank into a tableau of apocalyptic carnage.

"Do you believe this surprise attack idea of yours south of the battlefront will work?" General Timoshyn asked his Deputy in a low, shaking voice. His eyes were expressionless but behind his grim façade his mind was racing. He turned and glanced at the devastation littered along the banks of the Oder as the last American Warthog disappeared to the west.

"Yes," Stavatesky said gravely.

"Would you stake your reputation and career on it?" Timoshyn turned and fired off the question.

That made the Deputy CINC-West balk. He sensed a trap, and his voice lowered and softened. "Yes." He felt compelled.

The general nodded through the haze of smoke, then pronounced like a judge delivering a verdict. "Very well. Then you will lead the attack personally, Deputy Stavatesky. You have twenty-four hours to finalize your plans."

Stavatesky blinked through an appalled moment of utter astonishment and then finally found his voice.

"But my General," he gasped. "We are talking about a small attack, many miles away from the real battlefront. A lowly major, or even a captain could execute such a manoeuvre. Surely, I am more valuable to the army here, at your side, where the fighting will be fiercest."

General Timoshyn's eyes turned flinty, and his voice became brutal. "Don't you want to be the man who single-handledly wins the war for the Motherland, Deputy Stavatesky? A successful assault that turns the tide of the fight on the western front would make you a hero of the Russian Federation and catapult you into the upper echelons of political power."

That realization brought another pause, this time longer. The general had understood that Stavatesky was an ambitious man and had baited him with the tantalizing prospect of glory and adoration.

"Very well," Stavatesky nodded, conceding his lust for power. "I will win the war for the Motherland, my General."

*

The two understrength battalions of infantry to be used for the surprise outflanking attack were drawn from the 35th Separate Guards Motor Rifle Brigade, and the vehicles that would carry the troops to glory were pre-historic BTR-50s. The Deputy CINC-West looked aghast for a long moment at the mottled collection of APCs, and then shrugged with resignation. The BTRs were tracked amphibious personnel carriers that had entered service with the Soviet Army back in the 1950s. Lightly armored and packing a KPVT heavy machine gun, the vehicles were relics that had been shipped to the western front to replace some of the hundreds of modern BMPs that had been destroyed in the first weeks of the fighting. The BTR-50 was served by a two-man crew and could each transport twelve troops.

The soldiers were another disappointment for Stavatesky. The eight hundred men he had been allotted from the 35th Separate Guards had been fighting on the front line since the fall of Warsaw. They were wilting with exhaustion, standing with bovine resignation in ragged ranks, their uniforms mismatched and filthy with grime, their eyes on the ground, their shoulders slumped with the suffering resignation of men who had seen too much horror to care anymore.

Stavatesky inspected the men, walking silent and sullen between the ranks, noting the dull expressions on the men's half-starved faces. Finally, he came to a halt mid-stride and lifted his voice.

"Brave sons of Russia, I am Deputy Commander-In-Chief West, General Oleg Stavatesky. For the next few days, I am honored to be your acting commander. Together, we are going to win the war for the Motherland. Together, we are going to turn the tide on the western front and outsmart our enemies. Together, we are going to win a victory for Russia that will be remembered forever as the turning point of the war. Tomorrow, we advance on the enemy. Our victory is assured."

It was a stirring speech. Stavatesky saw a few men in the front ranks shuffle their feet and straighten their backs.

Good, he thought. The men still have some fighting spirit in them. Not enough to put fear into the hearts of a crack allied infantry unit – but enough to deal with a small village of frightened elderly German peasants.

Of that, he was certain.

POTSDAM, GERMANY

Chapter 1:

When he had retired from the US Army Special Forces as a Lieutenant Colonel a decade earlier, the very last thing Frank Purcell had ever expected was to find himself back in uniform – and back at war.

He had enlisted in the 1980's and served for twelve years on active duty before joining the Reserves for a further ten years. He had seen combat action in Africa, Grenada, Panama and the Middle East, and been wounded twice. When he had left the army and taken on security contracting work, he had thought his days of blood and guts and glory were past him. Now, at age sixty, he was once again in harm's way, fighting on the front lines for Europe's freedom. His uniform was a little tight around his stocky frame, and perhaps his reflexes weren't as sharp as they had been when he was in his prime. His hair had silvered, and his mustache was struck through with strands of grey – but his instincts were still razor sharp.

He stared out through the office window, peering across the vast stretch of concrete runway, his dark intelligent eyes deeply set within a web of wrinkled sun-browned skin and his brow was furrowed with consternation. Purcell was a man who didn't like surprises, and the news of this imminent visit had put all his instincts on edge.

"It can't be for anything good," he muttered darkly to his XO, sitting on the opposite side of the desk. "Mr. Devereaum doesn't make unscheduled visits unless it's for a significant reason. Are the Devils assembled? Is everything ship-shape?"

The Devil's Detail was a company-strength security force of armed contractors, hired to protect Devereaum Holding assets in Germany. The unit was made up of retired army veterans drawn from around the world; old war horses who had returned to combat for one last mission. Most of the men were Americans, but there were others from France, Australia, Canada and the UK who had been lured back into uniform either by the promise of financial reward or because of a patriotic calling. They were all too old for the Big Army, but not too old to fight.

The Devil's Detail was a PMC (Private Military Company), operating in Europe with the German Government's permission. Kyle Devereaum, the unit's financier and benefactor, was a Texan billionaire industrialist with a dozen munition factories scattered throughout the German countryside. When war had broken out in Europe, Devereaum had sought out Purcell and given him the task of gathering a force of combat experienced mercenaries to defend his installations.

The unit had assembled in Heidelberg just as Russian troops had seized Warsaw. Now, with the Russians massing on Germany's eastern border and threatening to drive towards Berlin, Purcell and the Devil's Detail were in Potsdam, a few miles southwest of the capital, defending Devereaum's main ordinance factory and facing the bleak threat of imminent action.

During the past two nights, Russian bombers and missiles had struck Berlin and caused fear and chaos amongst the German population. Many Berliners had begun evacuating the capital, streaming westward, choking every road out of the city. Frank Purcell had no doubt that if the Russians continued their bombing attacks, it would only be a matter of time before the enemy turned its sights on Devereaum's military installation.

"The men are ready," Purcell's XO said. "They're assembling as we speak out on the verge of the helipad."

Tom Hawker was a retired major in his fifties. He had served in the army for over twenty years, predominately as a tanker commanding an M1A1 Abrams. He had seen combat action in Operation Desert Shield, Operation Desert Storm and Operation Iraqi Freedom before retiring thirteen years earlier. A tall black man with an ageless face and an unshakable calmness under pressure, Hawker was also a new grandfather with a wife, three sons and a newborn grandchild waiting anxiously for him back in Louisville, Kentucky. Purcell had personally hand-picked Hawker as his second-in-command and Hawker had felt roused by a band-of-brothers stirring of patriotic duty. The two men were not close friends, but they had an easy relationship of trust and mutual respect because they recognized in each other the qualities they admired most in veteran soldiers.

The distant, unmistakable sound of an approaching helicopter brought both officers promptly from Purcell's makeshift headquarters.

They stepped out into the pale afternoon gloom and peered north towards a lead-grey bank of low cloud.

The AgustaWestland AW139 came clattering towards the helipad, low over the rooftops, hanging in the air for several seconds before landing neatly in a dust storm of downdraft. The cabin door opened as the rotors began to spool down and then a set of steps appeared at the entryway. After a brief moment Kyle Devereaum emerged.

Kyle Devereaum was a tall, middle-aged Texan with the gangling uncoordinated movements of someone awkward in his own skin. But his physical limitations were more than made up for by a towering intellect and his engineering genius. He was a brilliant innovator, and notoriously eccentric. He came clumping down the helicopter's steps with a charismatic smile on his face and gripped Frank Purcell's hand firmly.

"Good to see you, Frank. Tom," he acknowledged Hawker standing at the Lieutenant Colonel's side. "Thanks for making time to meet with me."

That last statement was the measure of Kyle Devereaum; effusively polite and modest, he worked hard to put the people he employed at ease.

"No trouble at all, sir," Purcell said impulsively.

Devereaum flicked a glance past Purcell's shoulder and ran his eye over the assembled troops. "Mind if I take a moment to chat to some of the boys before we huddle up?"

"Not at all," Purcell smiled dutifully, then flicked a wary glance at the Devil's Detail, paraded along the edge of the helipad. The troops were kitted out in procured US Army uniforms and equipment so that at a passing glance they looked like any other assembly of grunts – until a closer inspection revealed their aged faces and the distinctive patch on their right shoulders. The US flag had been replaced with the emblem of a red-faced devil bearing white horns and sporting a sinister, mocking grin.

Some of the men were grey-haired and middle-aged. Some, like Hawker, were grandfathers. Some of the men were bald and haggard from life's indulgences. But they were all veteran combat soldiers with nearly two millennia of fighting experience between them.

Devereaum shared a few minutes of raucous banter with the men, moving easily between them with a smile and an affable 'howdy' while Purcell and Hawker watched on. When Deveraux returned, he was grinning easily as if he didn't have a worry in the world.

"Right," he said, his demeanor changing in an instant. "Let's find a quiet place to talk. I've got news and orders for you – and there's a ticking clock on the job."

*

Frank Purcell spread a map of the German border across his desk and the three men gathered close together. Kyle Devereaum thrust his hands deep into his trouser pockets and rocked back on the balls of his feet.

"I've just come from a high-level meeting in Berlin with the President of Germany, the President of the Bundestag, and the German Chancellor," Devereaum began. "They're worried. The ease with which the Russian forces seized Poland has them deeply concerned, and the air and missile attacks that struck Berlin over the past two nights have shaken their confidence in the ability of the allied armies to hold the border. They're ordering a mandatory evacuation from the capital and all the major cities close to the Oder. Over the next few days, the road networks are going to be choked with refugees fleeing the warzone."

Tom Hawker nodded. Civilian casualties during the first bloody weeks of the war had been appalling. In Poland alone, up to a million non-combatants were either listed as dead or missing. "That's a sensible move," he approved of the German government's order. "My bet is that the air attacks on Berlin are only going to intensify."

"Yes," Devereaum agreed. "That's what the Chancellor thinks. But it raises a more immediate problem for Devereaum Holdings. I have people – good people, working in my munition facilities across the country. These are American citizens: designers, engineers, scientists... some of them are in harm's way."

"You want us to organize an evacuation for your plant here in Potsdam?" Frank Purcell guessed.

"No. That's already been taken care of as part of the government's general evacuation order for the residents of Berlin," Devereaum shook his head and then sucked in a sharp, ominous breath. "I have a much more pressing problem. I have people here," he leaned over the table and pressed his thumbnail into the map. "It's a sleepy little hamlet ten miles south of the battlefront but within a few short miles of the Polish border. There are eighty-three Americans there; Devereaum employees and their families. I need them transported west to safety. I need you and the Devil's Detail to go and fetch them before the fighting intensifies and all hell breaks loose."

Purcell and Hawker peered hard at the map. The small village was nestled close to the banks of the Western Neisse River which flowed north from the Czech border before eventually spilling into the Oder. The settlement sat huddled around a highway intersection.

"Klein Gastrose? I've never heard of the place," Purcell frowned.

"There's no reason for you to know it," Devereaum agreed. "It's a quiet little village, but it's also home to a small Devereaum Holdings design office."

"Who are these employees?" Frank Purcell frowned. "What kind of work do they do? I don't recall you having a munitions factory anywhere close by."

"No, there are no factory workers in the village. The staff working at Klein Gastrose are designers and engineers, mainly. They're innovating components for gyroscopic navigation equipment that can be used in the next generation of US missile systems. They work from a building on the outskirts of the hamlet."

"Eighty-three people, you say?" Tom Hawker began turning his mind to the logistics of an evacuation.

"Yes. Thirty-nine are direct employees. The others are their wives, husbands and children."

Frank Purcell shot Hawker a quick, meaningful glance, then straightened, his mind already wrestling with the practicalities of the problem.

"We're going to need trucks," he said.

"Already taken care of," Kyle Devereaum answered smoothly. "The German government has provided eight MAN KAT-1 military off-road transport trucks, and I have procured three surplus UN Toyota LandCruisers. They're being re-painted. Everything should be arriving here before nightfall."

"Ammunition?"

"Enough to fight your own private war," Devereaum said. "You'll have all the rounds you need for the men's M4s, as well as grenades and radio equipment. And I've also provided four FGM-148 Javelins with reloads. Everything will arrive with the trucks."

"Damn," Tom Hawker gave a small grunt of appreciation. "That's quite an investment of resources for an evacuation."

Devereaum shrugged. "It's only money and influence," he said dismissively. "The people in that hamlet are priceless. I want them kept safe at all costs."

"When do we leave?" Purcell needed to know.

"Tomorrow morning at dawn," Kyle Devereaum said. "You need to be on the road and heading south before the government declares the emergency civilian evacuation orders for Berlin and the highways fill with panicking refugees."

*

Purcell and Hawker strode into the factory's dining room after the completion of the evening meal. The Devils were spread amongst the tables, finishing their dinner. Some were slouched back, reading. Others were clustered together in small groups playing cards. A few were smoking and drinking quietly.

Purcell stepped to the front of the room and climbed up onto a table to get the men's attention.

"Alright, listen up," he propped his hands on his hips and cast a slow scan about the room to be sure everyone was heeding him. Although the Devil's Detail was structured and equipped at a platoon level much the same as a regular US Army company, discipline was far less formal. These men weren't fresh-faced raw recruits new to war. They were veterans who deserved respect. Purcell treated the troops like men and trusted them.

"We've got a job and it's an important one," Purcell explained. The men had eyes on him now, their faces intrigued with curiosity. "We're heading out at sunrise tomorrow morning. There's a little village south of Guben called Klein Gastrose where eighty-three American employees of Devereaum Holdings and their families are stationed. Our job is to get them west to safety before the fighting along the western front kicks off. Any questions?"

"How are we supposed to evacuate them?" a slim, grey-bearded man sitting at one of the nearby tables asked the question.

"The German Army is providing eight trucks."

"Only eight? Mate, that's going to make for a tight fucking fit," a man from the back of the room spoke, his speech slow, his tone a nasal twang. He was an Australian who had served in the SAS. He sat, lounged indolently in his chair, with a bottle of German beer resting balanced on the small paunch of his stomach. "A hundred of our mob and eighty weeping shit-scared bloody office-workers is too many for just eight transports. But, in the name of duty and sacrifice, I'm happy to let one of the pretty secretaries sit on my lap if it helps."

Some of the men nearby laughed and for a moment the meeting threatened to break out into bawdy banter. Frank Purcell held up his hand to stifle the moment.

"Yes, Bluey, you have a point," he answered the Australian. "It might be crowded, but we'll have to make do as best we can. We'll also have a few LandCruisers in the convoy and maybe we can make use of some civilian transport around the village if we need it. The important thing is that we get to Klein Gastrose and get out again as smoothly and as quickly as possible. The Russians are in a mood, and they've already begun launching air and missile attacks across the border. Any moment the entire front could go up in flames and the shooting will start."

"Are you expecting trouble, Frank?" another man asked from a table against the far wall of the room. He was a former US infantryman who had completed three tours of duty in Iraq and had fought at the Second Battle of Fallujah. He had a drawn, studious face and dark eyes, sunk deep into their sockets.

"No," Purcell said and meant it. He shook his head. "This is a precaution, that's all. Every piece of intelligence the allies have gathered suggests that the Russians are going to attack somewhere around Bad Freienwalde within the next forty-eight hours. We'll be a long way from the fighting."

Some of the tension went out of the room. Men relaxed. None of them relished the notion of combat. They were all prepared for the possibility, but they weren't gung-ho naïve recruits, enamored with Hollywood's stylized version of battle. Many of them were family men with wives and children back home. They knew first-hand that a firefight was bloody and terrifying and brutal. They had taken Devereaum money as mercenary contractors, and they realized the deal came with the very real risk of warfare – but they weren't the kind of men to go seeking trouble just for suicidal thrills.

"What about kit?" another voice asked from somewhere at the back of the room where the faces were obscured by a veil of drifting cigarette and cigar smoke.

"All the ammo and grenades we could possibly ever need... and four Javelins," Purcell said, and the men whooped with boyish delight and applause. Most of them were gun-aficionados who knew their weapons.

"Shit, yeah!" someone hollered. "Some red-blooded, red-necked American whoop-ass if the Ruskies want to get nasty with us. I feel better about this job already."

Another round of banter washed through the dining room and this time Purcell indulged it, smiling along with the jokes and the bravado until Tom Hawker glanced down at his watch.

"Okay! Enough!" he shouted down the burble of voices with the stern tone of a schoolmaster. "We move out at oh-five hundred hours tomorrow morning. Any man not locked and loaded and waiting by the helipad gets docked a month's salary."

*

Not for the first time, Frank Purcell checked his watch in the pre-dawn darkness. It was still fifteen minutes before the convoy of trucks and LandCruisers were due for departure. He glanced down the long line of vehicles, glowing under the compound's flood lights, then beckoned Tom Hawker to his side.

Here's the order of vehicles," he said, counting off on his fingers as he spoke. "I want a LandCruiser at the head of the convoy carrying four armed men to run interference. I will be in the second LandCruiser with a driver. Then I want First Platoon in the two lead trucks, followed by Second Platoon and Third Platoon, each in two of the trucks. The last two trucks in the convoy will be kept for ammunition and equipment. You will bring up the rear with a driver in the third LandCruiser. Make sense?"

"Sure," Hawker nodded.

"And we stay in radio contact until we reach Klein Gastrose."

"Roger that."

Hawker disappeared for a few moments and returned from the dining room with two mugs of coffee. He handed one to Purcell and the two men stood quietly and companionably sipping at the steaming liquid while the last of the Devils emerged from their barracks and took their place in the lines of waiting troops. The truck engines were idling, filling the pre-dawn air with belching diesel fumes. One of the men walked past and Purcell called to him.

"Bluey! I want you in the second LandCruiser with me. You can drive, right?"

"Ever since I was old enough to steal a car," the Australian said laconically.

Purcell nodded.

Hawker took another sip of his coffee then went down the line of troops, handpicking the men to ride in the lead Toyota and the drivers for the rest of the vehicles.

"One platoon between each two trucks," he barked instructions to the men. "Sort yourselves out. One platoon between every two trucks."

Frank Purcell checked his watch again. "Fuck it," he grumbled. Patience wasn't his strong suit and departing a few minutes early would only get them to their destination sooner. "Mount up!" he shouted above the rumble of the truck engines. "Devil's Detail, mount up!"

They clambered aboard the vehicles. No one spoke. The lieutenants leading each platoon sorted their men with quiet efficiency and within a matter of minutes everyone was aboard and ready for departure. Frank Purcell walked down the line of vehicles.

"All set?"

"All set," the men in each truck replied.

Purcell returned to the lead Toyota. He leaned through the open window on the driver's side.

"You guys are on point," he peered into the faces of the four men Hawker had selected for the task, "so keep your eyes open and your wits about you. There might be roadblocks south of the city and enemy missile damage." Each of the three men in the passenger seats had their M4s between their knees and were listening to him attentively with serious faces. "Keep your speed to forty and keep in radio comms. Don't get too far ahead of the convoy and don't run any risks."

The convoy pulled out through the gates of the factory plant with engines revving in low gear and headlights burning. Purcell had deliberately chosen a route that would take them southwards through back roads. It was a less-direct path than making use of the highway network, but he figured it would be a safer bet. Every route leading north towards Berlin had been choked for days with convoys of troops and tanks being rushed towards the brewing battlefront, and if the Russians decided to launch an air attack on one of those convoys, he wanted to be as far away from the carnage as possible.

For the first few miles they headed east, towards the border, and then the trucks turned off onto a side road for the journey south. They cleared the outskirts of Potsdam just as the sun was rising over their left shoulders. The new day had dawned bleak and grey with low cloud so that the drizzle-misted landscape looked soft as an impressionist painting.

Purcell allowed himself a brief moment to relax. He checked the vehicle's rear mirror to reassure himself that the convoy of heavy trucks was following then gave his mind over to calculations. Typically, the journey would be a comfortable three-hour drive in a family sedan. Purcell figured he'd added an extra hour of traveling time to the trip because of his chosen circuitous route; maybe an hour-and-a-half, taking into account the slow speed of the trucks. Still, they should be arriving in Klein Gastrose well before midday. That would allow them two hours to gather together the Devereaum staff and then another three or four hours of daylight to drive west towards Leipzig and relative safety. Once they were well away from the border, the Devereaum employees would be airlifted out of Germany, and the Devil's Detail would return to Potsdam to resume their security work – unless the Russians broke through the allied lines and Berlin fell – which was a distinct possibility.

Like most other keen military observers, Purcell too had been impressed and astonished by the speed at which the Russian army had swept west since the outbreak of war, gobbling up vast tracts of Poland seemingly with ease. The Russians, it appeared on the surface, were unstoppable, and he figured the German government were right to be concerned. If the allied armies gathered along the banks of the Oder could not hold back the tide of Russian tanks and troops, all of eastern Germany would be overrun.

He wondered what defeat for the allies might mean for him and his men, and then suddenly Bluey in the driver's seat was talking, dragging him back to the present.

The Australian had a cigarette dangling from the corner of his mouth as he spoke around puffs of smoke.

"I reckon you're gonna need to get on the radio, boss," Bluey pointed ahead through the windshield. "Looks like the Germans have a roadblock up ahead. You might want to tell the boys in the lead vehicle not to open fire," he joked.

Purcell peered past the lead Toyota and saw a camouflaged German Army Boxer AFV parked across the far end of the road and a cluster of uniformed German Feldjägers standing in front of the vehicle. The Bundeswehr MPs were peering suspiciously towards the approaching convoy, and as the vehicles drew closer, one of the Germans held up his hand, ordering a halt.

Purcell lunged for the radio clipped to his belt and thumbed the button to transmit. "Slow down! Slow down!" he spoke urgently to the driver in the lead Toyota. "Stop a hundred yards short of the roadblock and tell everyone in that vehicle to keep their hands well away from their weapons."

The convoy ground to a halt and the Feldjägers stood their ground, not moving. Bluey knocked the LandCruiser out of gear and left the engine idling.

"Want me to come with you?" the big Australian offered with willing eagerness.

"Christ, no!" Purcell almost choked at the thought. The big Australian was just as likely to insult the MPs with a torrent of foul-mouthed abuse and start a brawl. "You stay right here and don't do anything. And keep your mouth shut."

Purcell kicked open the passenger door and climbed out of the vehicle. He got on comms to Tom Hawker.

"We've struck a German roadblock," he explained to his XO. "Tell all the boys in the trucks to sit tight while I sort things out."

He lit a cigarette with nonchalant indifference and strode confidently towards the waiting German MPs. When he was twenty paces from the nearest Feldjäger, the man called out sharply, "Who are you and what is your business on this road?"

Purcell never faltered, nor did the calm smile on his face slip. He dropped the cigarette onto the road and stomped on it. "I am retired US Army Lieutenant Colonel Frank Purcell," he said, his eyes roaming across the faces of the German sentries. "I am commanding a PMC named the Devil's Detail. We are employed by Devereaum Holdings. We're on a rescue mission with orders to travel south to Klein Gastrose to evacuate eighty-three American civilians and transport them west to Leipzig," he explained everything patiently.

The Germans remained unfriendly, unsmiling and suspicious.

"You have authorization?" the *Leutnant* commanding the detail had a sharp voice and a thick German accent that made the question sound more like an accusation.

"I have papers," Purcell confirmed, and reached into the pocket of his uniform. He had two official letters; one from Kyle Devereaum and another from the Secretary of the Office of the German Chancellor. He unfolded the papers and handed them across to the German officer.

The *Leutnant* turned the documents towards the morning light to read them, then grunted. "How many men are in those trucks?" he pointed to the stalled convoy.

"A company."

"Weapons?"

"M4s and a couple of Javelins."

"Explosives?"

Purcell shook his head. "No. Just grenades."

The *Leutnant* turned on his heel and withdrew to the Boxer AFV. Purcell stood in the middle of the road, feeling vulnerable and cruelly exposed. The MPs were tense and alert, their fingers on the triggers of their weapons.

After a few minutes the Feldjäger *Leutnant* returned, his face a dour pale mask of severity. "Very well," he conceded. "Your papers are valid, and your mission has been confirmed. But you should be warned that the roads into and out of Berlin are being patrolled all the way south to Dresden, and you travel at your own risk. Air alerts along the border have been raised, and Russian fighter jets have been spotted on radar just over the border."

"Thank you," Purcell said politely. He stuffed the documents back into the pocket of his tunic. "We'll be careful."

The *Leutnant* barked an order, and the men moved to the side of the road. The Boxer's big engine rumbled to life and the AFV reversed, clearing the route. Purcell walked confidently back to the lead LandCruiser.

"Take is slow and steady for the next couple of miles, and keep your guns out of sight. The Germans are edgy, and I don't want to give them an excuse to fill us full of holes, okay?"

The convoy trundled sedately on through the countryside. The morning brightened and patches of blue sky slowly emerged. The road they were on veered south west past green pastures and small villages and then snaked back towards the border. Bluey reached under the driver's seat of the Toyota and handed Purcell a warm bottle of German beer. "Drink? All this driving is thirsty work," the Australian said.

"Are you out of your mind?" Purcell looked appalled. "Throw that out the window. I want you sober as a judge until we're back in Potsdam."

The Australian looked crestfallen. He flung the beer bottle grudgingly out through the open window like he was farewelling a beloved relative, then fell into a sulking silence for the next hour.

In the middle of the morning Purcell got back on comms to the lead vehicle. "There's a village coming up," he could see the spire of a church in the far distance, his view of other buildings partly obscured by a fringe of verdant trees. "Drive on through and then look for a place to stop once we're back on a stretch of open road."

*

The lead LandCruiser blew through the little German village and two miles later pulled suddenly onto the gravel shoulder of the road, kicking up a cloud of dust. Purcell got on the radio to the following procession of trucks. "We're pulling over."

The convoy peeled off the road and eased to a stop with a wall of green forest beside them.

"Everybody out. You've got ten minutes to stretch your legs."

The men spilled from the trucks and milled around by the roadside. Some lit cigarettes. Most wandered into the nearby fringe of trees to piss. Purcell and Hawker came together. Purcell checked his watch and winced.

"We're behind schedule," he muttered.

Tom Hawker had a folded map clutched in his hand. He ran his finger over the route and made a guess. "I'd say we're still two hours from our destination."

Purcell grunted, and cast a glance around him. The trucks were parked at the start of a long straight stretch of two-lane road, bordered on both side by thick forest. They were in a shallow valley, surrounded by low hills. Overhead the sky had turned dark and foreboding once more, the heavy grey clouds threatening rain.

Purcell felt a twinge of eerie premonition and frowned.

A family sedan appeared in the distance, coming closer at speed. There was something about the erratic nature of the vehicle that aroused Purcell's suspicion. He watched the car come closer and realized it was towing a trailer, stacked high with household belongings. On an impulse, he stepped out into the middle of the road.

The car reluctantly braked to a halt opposite the convoy and Purcell strode towards the driver's side window. The car's engine was still revving. The driver was an elderly German man with an old woman in the passenger seat. The car radio was blaring, broadcasting news in German.

"I am Lieutenant Colonel Frank Purcell," he introduced himself politely. The elderly driver's face was tight with agitation, his hands white-knuckled on the steering wheel. "Can you tell me how far it is to Klein Gastrose?"

"What?" the old man spoke thickly accented English. "Klein Gastrose?"

"Yes. How far away is it?"

"Christ! Are you crazy, man?" the German blurted. "Hasn't your American army got radios? Haven't you heard the news?"

"What news?" Purcell's expression tightened and something oily slithered and knotted in his guts.

The German turned up the car radio.

"I don't speak German," Purcell explained, wincing. "Please turn that thing off."

The man killed the radio. The woman began weeping softly.

"The Russian Army has begun its attack along the western front," the old man said in a wheeze of exasperation. "Their tanks and soldiers have pushed across the border and are assaulting Wriezen and there have been air strikes up and down the entire front. Bad Freienwalde has already fallen and the allies in the area are being pushed back. The government is broadcasting an emergency evacuation order. We must leave our homes and flee west immediately."

"Shit," Purcell muttered. He turned to look for Tom Hawker and in that moment of distraction the elderly German gunned his engine and sped away.

Purcell relayed the news to his XO and the two men dashed to Purcell's Toyota. They tuned the vehicle's radio to BBC and listened as a rush of breaking news flashes filled in the grim picture. The Russians had launched their attack an hour earlier, preceded by an artillery barrage. The French infantry defending the sector had been pushed back and now British tanks and troops were being rushed forward in an attempt to stem the Russian incursion. Purcell and Hawker exchanged troubled glances.

Purcell turned the radio off. "Get everyone back into the trucks," he said.

They spilled from the Toyota and began barking orders. Another car flashed past them, heading west, and then two more, each sagging low on its suspension with the weight of hastily-packed personal belongings. Soon, Purcell knew, the road would be choked and people panicked.

Then suddenly a troubling sound made Frank Purcell stop and pause. It was an ethereal noise, seeming to float and waver on the wind. He cast his eyes towards the low cloud, searching, and then saw a tiny flash of reflected light far away in the east, coming quickly closer. He peered for another long moment and a dark spec appeared low in the sky.

"Incoming air attack!" he cupped his hands to his mouth and bellowed. "Everyone get into the trees and take cover!"

The Russian SU-25 dropped out of the clouds, flying at barely a hundred feet off the ground, jinking erratically in flight as it swooped towards the line of stationary trucks. Purcell felt his blood turn to ice.

The men who were milling idly around the tailgates of the trucks suddenly broke apart and scattered into the nearby woods. Purcell stood and stared at the approaching enemy ground attack jet, and then saw a second dark spec emerge from the clouds, cutting through the air like a dart in pursuit.

Tom Hawker dashed out into the middle of the road and seized Purcell's arm. "Jesus, Frank! Get your ass into cover!"

The two men ran like startled jackrabbits for the nearest trees as the SU-25 bore down on the convoy. Purcell hit the ground hard and then looked up just in time to see the Russian jet clearly. It was flying low to the ground, following the line of the road, jinking in the air as the F-16 behind it closed inexorably.

The enemy pilot saw the line of parked military trucks and, despite being hunted and just moments away from death, he opened fire. The air shuddered and filled with the scream of high-powered jet engines followed by the thundering roar of heavy machine gun fire. The second KAT-1 in the line suddenly shook and then the vehicle's windshield exploded into a million glittering shards of glass. The front of the truck dissolved to a blur of shuddering bullet strikes and then a soft whoosh of drumming flames engulfed the vehicle.

The Russian Frogfoot flashed overhead, and then banked violently to the right. The F-16 pilot in pursuit saw the enemy jet turn directly across his gun sights and opened fire. A moment later the Russian SU-25 became engulfed in a thundering fireball of flames. It fell from the sky, raining jagged debris across the forest, and crashed somewhere beyond the veil of trees. The F-16 flashed past and then started to climb. Within seconds it had disappeared into the clouds.

Purcell and Hawker emerged from cover, stunned but compelled by urgency.

"Move those other trucks!" Hawker barked quick orders before the flames could spread to the remaining seven transports.

The burning KAT-1 was a write-off. Thick oily smoke drifted across the road and spilled into the sky. The fierce heat of the flames started to melt the metal chassis. The vehicle sagged down on one side and small brush fires ignited along the forest's edge. Purcell stood with his hands on his hips, impotent with helplessness and watched the truck turn to ashes.

He took the setback with bleak regret, but acceptance. In combat some factors were beyond a commander's control. The only way to keep moving forward was to adapt to the variables and overcome the obstacles.

"Get the men back onto the remaining trucks," he told Hawker. "Cram them in like sardines if you have to. We're moving out in five minutes."

Chapter 2:

The road ahead of the convoy twisted and turned through the German countryside, taking them past farm fields, patches of lush forest and small isolated villages. Purcell kept one eye on his watch and the other on the sky, wary of further Russian attack jets that might burst through the low cloud cover without warning.

At mid-morning they reached a road juncture that intersected a main north-south highway. All four lanes of the freeway were jammed with allied tanks, trucks and troops heading north towards the warzone beneath a drifting cloud of diesel exhaust.

Purcell's radio crackled to life.

"Roadblock five hundred yards ahead," the driver in the lead LandCruiser spoke quickly.

"Germans?" Purcell wanted to know.

"I think they're our guys."

"Slow to a stop a hundred paces short of the barrier."

The convoy braked to a halt in the middle of the road and Purcell climbed from his vehicle. "Tom, come with me," he spoke on comms to Hawker in the vehicle at the rear of the column.

The two men went forward together. The roadblock consisted of two US Army M1117 security vehicles each armed with a grenade launcher and a 50 caliber M2HB heavy machine gun. Behind the two armored vehicles were three Humvees and a crew of a dozen Army MPs.

"Jesus," Hawker rubbed at the stubble on his chin in a moment of surprise. "They're not kidding, are they?"

It was a substantial and intimidating presence. Purcell and Hawker approached the vehicles, and an MP stepped forward.

The female sergeant commanding the roadblock eyed Hawker and Purcell with a police officer's instinctive suspicion.

"Are you two gentlemen lost?" she noted the uniforms and then the distinctive devil's head badges on their right shoulders.

Purcell smiled a thin, patient smile. "No sergeant. We're on our way to Klein Gastrose on a rescue mission."

"Is that so?" the MP arched a curious eyebrow. "What's in the trucks?"

"Men and ammunition," Purcell said. "We're a PMC, employed by Devereaum Holdings, operating with the written permission of the German government," as he spoke, he reached into his tunic pocket and produced the same letters he had shown the Germans earlier in the morning.

The sergeant took the papers and read them. Twice.

"Why are you heading to Klein Gastrose?"

"Eighty-three American citizens and their families are stranded there. We have orders to get them to safety but we're on a tight schedule..." he let the last few words hang in the air for a moment. "We really need to get across this freeway as quickly as possible."

"How many men do you have?"

"A company."

The road behind them was choked with all manner of vehicles, most of them American. Purcell watched a column of Oshkosh M1070 transporters rumble past, each towing a semi-trailer bearing an Abrams battle tank. The procession took several minutes to blow by and was followed by a line of M1126 Stryker combat vehicles. Behind them, and stretching as far south as Purcell could see, were supply trucks and Humvees and even a column of what looked like German Boxer RCH-155 self-propelled howitzers.

Purcell tried a different approach. He took a step closer to the sergeant and lowered his voice to a confidential mutter. "Look, I realize the world is a few minutes away from going to hell, but I have over eighty American civilians waiting for me and my men to rescue them. They're innocent people, caught up in the conflict and my company is made up of about a hundred FOGS (fucking old guys) like us two," he turned to include Hawker. "At our age, we need to be tucked up in bed with a warm cup of milk by nineteen hundred hours, so we can take our heart meds and our blood-pressure pills. So, can you cut us old guys a break?"

The sergeant didn't want to smile, but she did. She tossed Purcell a lop-sided grin, then nodded her head. "Have your trucks ready, sir," she used the honorific in respectful deference to Purcell's age, rather than his rank. "And when I give you the signal, you go like bats out of hell, straight across the freeway. Understand?"

Purcell smiled and nodded his thanks. The two men jogged back to their vehicles and Purcell got on comms to every driver.

"Engines idling and be ready to go when we get the word," he spoke quickly, then nodded to Bluey. "Don't jerk around once we get the all-clear, otherwise we could be stranded here for days."

The column sat idling on the blacktop for another two minutes like they were on a starting grid, waiting for the green flag. Then the two M1117s suddenly reversed, and the MPs waved them through.

"Go!" Purcell barked on the radio. The LandCruisers dashed forward with Bluey driving like a maniac, and then one-by-one the trucks crossed the freeway and jounced back down onto the far side, re-joining the access road. Hawker's trailing LandCruiser breezed by just before the lead Puma in a convoy of German IFVs reached the crossing point.

Purcell sat back in his seat and breathed a long sigh of relief, then checked his watch. "Put your foot down," he told Bluey. "We've got some serious time to make up and there are no more obstacles in our way."

*

Purcell was wrong.

Less than an hour from their destination the column became frustratingly slowed down by a tide of civilian vehicles fleeing westward, and then they encountered a US Army LRRP (Logistics Recovery and Replenishment Point) by the side of the road, bordered by a fringe of forest.

Frank Purcell didn't want to stop, but Tom Hawker made a compelling argument.

"We could do with some fuel, Frank," the XO made his case over the radio. "Maybe we could beg, borrow or steal some."

"We've got enough," Purcell dismissed the idea.

"We've got enough to reach Klein Gastrose," Hawker agreed. "But how far are we going to get once we start heading west to safety?"

Purcell grunted, then surrendered to logic. He grudgingly got on comms to the rest of the convoy. "Pull over. We're going to try to refuel at the LRRP."

The vehicles pulled off the road and into a grassy field. The ground had once been under the plow and was deeply rutted so that the heavy trucks rocked and swayed to a stop. Bluey parked the LandCruiser in the midst of the recovery point and killed the engine.

The field appeared like a scene of organized chaos. Part of it looked like a massive junk metal swap meet, with a dozen military vehicles sitting forlorn and abandoned beneath a fringe of trees, surrounded by scrap metal parts, engine blocks, and service trucks, including a massive M88A2 Hercules HRV (Heavy Recovery Vehicle). Purcell saw three broken-down Abrams M1 tanks in various stages of repair, their rakish lines spattered with mud and scratches and dents. Parked beside them were a handful of Strykers and Humvees, some disassembled down to their chassis, others suspended from hoists.

The opposite side of the field was given over to an array of tents for supplies, ammunition, medics, and catering, each surrounded by a number of parked service vehicles. Standing separate to the rest of the clutter and lined up close to the side of the road stood a small fleet of US Army HEMTT A4 fuel tankers waiting to be called into action.

Purcell set his eyes on the tankers and turned to Hawker. "Tom, unload the men. Let them stretch their legs for a few minutes, but tell them to stay close to the vehicles. I don't want anyone wandering off for free chow. I'm going to see if I can get some fuel."

He set out purposefully towards the line of fuel trucks but a voice from his left challenged him and Purcell turned, startled.

"Who the fuck are you?" the owner of the voice demanded. "And what the hell are you doing at my LRRP?"

Purcell turned and stared at a Lieutenant who stood with his hands on his hips, his tunic sleeves rolled up to his elbows and his forearms smeared with grease. Purcell flashed a friendly, slightly awkward smile, and went towards the officer with his hand outstretched. "Are you in charge here?"

"Yes, I am," the man introduced himself, still suspicious and on guard. "Lieutenant Jason Dunn, 1st Battalion 68th Armored Regiment, 4th Infantry Division. Now, I'll ask you one more time and then I'm going to shoot you. Who the fuck are you?"

"Howdy," Purcell made his tone amiable. "I'm retired Lieutenant Colonel Frank Purcell, commanding the Devil's Detail PMC," he went on to explain the purpose of his mission and the danger to the Devereaum Holding staff who were waiting for rescue. "My trucks need to be refuelled," he thrust his papers at Lieutenant Dunn and waited patiently while the young officer read them.

To his astonishment, the young officer shrugged and nodded. "That's fine by me," he said. "But make it quick. That fuel is for US Army fighting vehicles. We're not a local gas station."

Purcell thanked the Lieutenant profusely and jogged back to the convoy of troop transports, yelling orders as he went. The drivers mounted their vehicles, and the seven trucks trundled towards the refuellers, but to Purcell's dismay, Tom Hawker was missing. He cast a bewildered glance around the vast expanse of the field and suddenly spotted his XO standing atop the hull of one of the M1 Abrams tanks beneath the shade of the trees. Hawker was locked in an intense discussion with a couple of brawny army mechanics.

Purcell shook his head with a tolerant look of sympathetic dismay. Hawker had been a tanker for most of his twenty-one years of service. He had commanded Abrams tanks in battle throughout the Middle East. To Hawker, the Abrams was a beast of noble beauty.

The two young army mechanic corporals were listening to Hawker with bemused, indulgent smirks on their faces, clearly unaware that the tall middle-aged black man was an expert on the M1. One of the workers abruptly challenged Hawker and he smiled, baring his teeth and letting his voice harden just enough to make the mechanic flinch. "Son, I've been commanding and fighting these tanks since before you were an itch in your daddy's pants. I know them inside and out. I'm telling you the problem you've got with this tank is the hydraulic turret drive. That's why you're not getting a smooth traverse."

"You boys should listen to the man," Frank Purcell stood under the shade of a tree and lifted his face to the two mechanics, inserting himself into the discussion. "He knows what he's talking about. You're speaking to retired major Tom Hawker, a hero of Operation Desert Storm and one of the men who fought the famous Battle of 73 Easting."

The two young mechanics gawked in surprise and then glanced at Hawker with renewed respect. One of the corporals tried to stammer a profuse apology.

"I... I meant no disrespect, sir..."

Hawker blushed beneath his dark skin and Purcell took the opportunity to steal his XO away.

"Now, if you two hard-working mechanics will excuse us, my companion and I have a mission to complete and a ticking clock to beat," he fixed Hawker with a pointed stare.

*

The last thirty minutes of the drive to Klein Gastrose was on a stretch of smooth wide freeway and the convoy picked up speed, reaching the small village a few minutes before midday.

The settlement was a neat and tidy snapshot of German village life, nestled around a wide road junction. The route that ran through the village continued south towards the township of Forst and the intersecting left turn reached out towards the nearby Polish border. Most of the houses Purcell could see from the passenger window of the LandCruiser were humble, simple buildings, well maintained and brightly colored.

The shopfronts that lined the intersection were a mixture of local businesses, surrounded by a cluster of smaller buildings, all set against a backdrop of distant trees and rolling fields.

It was a place of tranquil serenity, lifted from a picture postcard or a tourism brochure.

"Looks like a pretty place," Bluey offered his opinion.

"The kind of little village a man might retire to," Purcell added.

He glanced at the road that branched off towards the border and studied it for a long moment of absent contemplation. The route was lined with tall leafy trees. About a hundred yards along the road stood another small cluster of shops, and a glass-fronted office block built in the shadow of a two-story hotel.

Purcell pointed. "That must be the Devereaum building," he guessed.

The convoy turned across the intersection and pulled up in front of the building. As the last truck braked to a halt a group of people spilled out through the glass doorway onto the sidewalk, waving and gesturing and smiling their gratitude and relief.

"I reckon that's a bingo," Bluey said. "They're the people we've come to rescue."

Purcell scanned the throng with a soldier's eye. About half of the crowd were female and most of them quite young. The men in the group were a more diverse mixture; some in their twenties and thirties but others were middle-aged. Standing amidst the group, but a little forward of the others, was a thin man in his thirties, dressed like a hipster. He had dark shaggy hair that he wore pulled up into a bun at the back of his head, the scruff of a beard across his chin, and wore black-rimmed glasses. The man had his hands thrust deep into his pockets, standing with restraint and composed authority. To one side of him stood an elderly white-haired man with a face crumpled by fear and anxiety. He was dressed in a threadbare suit and wearing a black tie.

Purcell climbed out of the LandCruiser and was joined on the sidewalk by Tom Hawker. Behind them, the Devil's Detail began the process of disembarking the trucks. Purcell strode directly towards the hipster with his hand outstretched and a tight smile on his face.

"You're Lieutenant Colonel Frank Purcell," the waiting man said.

"Yes."

"I'm Gary Wrexford, operations manager. Mr. Devereaum called last night to tell us you were coming. We're mightily relieved you're here," the two men shook hands.

Purcell introduced Tom Hawker and Wrexford introduced the elderly gentleman at his side.

"This is Herr Karl Heisse. He is kind of like the village mayor here in Klein Gastrose. He's very anxious for us all to begin the evacuation. We've been listening to the radio reports. The fighting that broke out around Bad Freienwalde this morning has a lot of the women concerned."

Purcell nodded, then flinched. He glanced at the elderly German and then back to Wrexford. "Just to be clear, Mr. Wrexford, my mission is to evacuate eighty-three American citizens – the employees and their families of Devereaum Holdings. You understand that, right?"

For a long, appalled moment Gary Wrexford did not answer, and then slowly, with color rising bright on his cheeks, he shook his head.

"No. We all have to be evacuated," he insisted stubbornly. "The villagers need to be escorted to safety too. They're our friends; they're like family to us."

Purcell did a double-take and felt his temper begin to fizz the blood in his veins. He turned to Tom Hawker, seething.

"XO, send two men with a radio towards the border," he snapped. "On the map there is a bridge across the Western

Neisse. Tell them to find a vantage point and tell them to keep their eyes open for trouble."

Hawker spun round and singled out two men for the task. They sped off down the freeway in one of the LandCruisers.

The precaution attended to, Purcell turned back to Wrexford. He was smiling, but there was no humor in his eyes. They were hard and cruel and ruthless.

"Listen to me carefully, Mr. Wrexford," he leaned menacingly close to the man. "I have clear orders from Kyle Devereaum. I'm only taking American company employees and their families. We have no room on the trucks to transport any German citizens. If they want to evacuate, they can use their own cars and make their own way west. They're not my problem, nor my responsibility. Now, you can either comply with my instructions, or you can stay here and put every one of your people's lives at risk."

Wrexford blanched like he had been slapped in the face, then turned apologetically to the elderly man and spoke quickly in German. The old man looked devastated. He glanced up at Purcell with rheumy eyes close to tears and launched into an impassioned appeal, pleading with his hands.

Purcell shook his head. "Tell him I can't help," he insisted, then checked his watch. This entire operation was quickly turning into a disaster. Purcell liked to be in control of every situation and this fiasco was on the verge of lurching towards mayhem.

He took a step back and turned his attention to the press of fearful faces gathered about him. Some of the women were weeping.

"We have seven trucks to transport you and your families to safety," he said. "You have two hours to return to your homes and collect your loved ones. Bring no personal possessions with you apart from important documents. No clothes, no pets. We are leaving here at exactly fourteen hundred hours. If you're not on a truck by then, you will be left behind."

It was an announcement delivered with harsh, brutal bluntness, but it was what the situation demanded.

Wrexford tried to protest, complaining that his staff needed more time, but Purcell cut the man off with a snarl. "This isn't a democracy, Mr. Wrexford. It's a rescue mission. Your hurt feelings will heal. Bullet wounds might not."

The crowd on the sidewalk dispersed, scampering for their cars, clutching their phones to their ears, calling their homes with breathless sobbing instructions for loved ones. Purcell and Hawker came together and considered the Devil's Detail. The men were clumped around the rear of each truck, talking quietly and smoking cigarettes. One of the men watched a pretty woman run past him and made a lewd laughing gesture to a companion.

"Find something useful for them to do," Purcell told Hawker with a twist of disdain. "I don't want them standing around ogling women, and I don't want to find them in a bar drinking."

Hawker nodded. "Bluey! Take a handful of men in a Toyota and do a recce around the outskirts of the village," the XO ordered. "I want to know about potential fields of fire and likely ambush positions. The rest of you men start stripping down your weapons, and after you've done that, we're going over each of the trucks piece by piece to check for mechanical issues. Now, move like you've got a purpose!"

*

NORTHEAST OF SEKOWICE, POLAND

The convoy of BTR-50s had travelled south from Gorzyca under the cover of darkness, using muddy, narrow back roads to remain inconspicuous and to avoid allied spy satellites. Progress was frustratingly slow in the dark, and the ancient APCs were well past their effective operational abilities. Four times during the night the convoy was forced to stop while running repairs were affected. By the time dawn light spilled across the western edge of Poland, six broken-down personnel carriers had been abandoned by the roadside.

General Stavatesky called a halt at sunrise and the long column of APCs ground to a weary stop. The General stepped stiffly from the interior of his BTR-80 command vehicle with a dark scowl on his face. He beckoned the major commanding the two battalions of riflemen towards him with a contemptuous thrust of his chin.

"We are still many miles from the border," Stavatesky growled, indicating a road sign that pointed towards the village of Biezyce. The launch point for the attack was the border settlement of Sekowice, a further eight kilometers southwest of their position.

"We must move faster."

"General, there is nothing more I can do," the hapless major flapped his arms in frustration. "Our equipment is shit. These BTR-50s are as old as my grandfather."

"They are all the Motherland can spare," the General bristled. "Or would you rather walk across the fucking border to fight your battle?"

The major blushed, chastened but still impotent to do anything other than make excuses. "Of course, you are right, General. I apologize if I sounded disloyal. I will have all the vehicles refueled immediately and ensure each one is ready for the final push into Poland."

"How long will it take?" Stavatesky growled.

The major winced. "An hour."

"Make it faster," the General fumed. He returned to his command vehicle and sat hunched beside his radio operator in the cramped, stinking confines of the BTR-80's interior. The radioman sat sweating at his controls.

"Tell me what is happening in the north," the General demanded.

The radioman snatched off his headphones and spoke quickly, his eyes darting and nervous.

"Our attacks across the border at Bad Freienwalde and Wriezen are pushing the enemy back," he reported. "The 90th Guards Tank Division has reached the outskirts of Wriezen and is driving forward, meeting some resistance but still gaining ground. Advance elements of the 150th Guards Motor Rifle Division are attacking Bad Freienwalde as we speak and are pushing the French back."

Stavatesky arched his bushy eyebrows in surprise. He felt deeply conflicted by the news. He had expected the attacks to be repulsed by the allies. If the advance did indeed break the back of the enemy, then Russian reserve units would pour through the gap and the entire allied front might collapse. That would make his own mission utterly redundant. Instead of being the General who single-handedly turned the tide of the war, he might instead be remembered as the senior officer who had been conspicuously absent at the moment of Russia's great military triumph. The ignominy, if such information ever leaked, would be the political death of him.

The news darkened Stavatesky's mood further and pricked at his impatience.

"What is happening in the air above the battlefield?" he gruffed.

"Details are conflicted," the radioman admitted. "Army West Command is reporting that several enemy F-16 fighters have been shot down and that our artillery is pounding British and American positions north and south of the conflict zone, inflicting heavy losses."

The General scoffed. Almost everything broadcast from Army West Command was propaganda, meant to bolster the flagging morale of the men in the trenches and to provide triumphant sound-bites for Russian State media. The trick to interpreting the transmissions was being able to discern the difference between the bullshit and brutal reality.

He halved the reported enemy losses and doubled the Russian losses and figured that was a fairer estimation of how the fight was developing. It was enough to give him a glimmer of ghoulish hope that perhaps the Russian offensive was not going anywhere near as smoothly as the radio suggested. He still had a chance to be the heroic figure of Russian folklore – if he could get the damned BTR-50s across the German border in time.

He lit a cigarette and puffed thoughtfully for a long moment. Beyond the walls of his command vehicle, he could hear the infantry major barking orders at his troops and then several engines began to rumble. Somewhere a junior officer swore bitterly with frustration and then bawled out a soldier for pissing against the steel side of a BTR-50.

"Go into the trees and do that, you filthy bastard!" the junior officer berated the soldier. "You're not a fucking animal."

It was all background noise to Stavatesky. He shut it out and let his thoughts pick at the details of his plan. Once he had secured Klein Gastrose, he knew that urgent action would be important. He would need tank support and air support to secure his prize and to threaten the southern flank of the enemy before the allies had time to react. That, he was sure, would be the key to triumph.

"I want you to keep the radio lines open to CINC-West Forward Command Post at all times from now until this mission ends," he told the radio operator. "I must remain in touch with General Timoshyn's senior staff at all costs. Do you understand this order, soldier?"

"Yes, General," the radio operator jerked his head and felt a bead of sweat run down his pale cheek.

"Good," Stavatesky snarled. "Because if you fail me – if I can't get the General on the radio the instant I need him – I will personally tie you naked to the front of this vehicle and cut off your fucking balls with a blunt hunting knife."

*

The column of Russian APCs reached the great roundabout that bypassed the Polish township of Sekowice in the middle of the morning and continued southwest to a vast concrete clearway that was an abandoned border crossing point, set close to the banks of the Neisse. Here the road narrowed to three lanes across the Lusatian Neisse Bridge.

General Stavatesky ordered the column to stop. He stepped from his command vehicle and with the infantry major at his side, the two men went forward towards a small rise of ground clutching high-powered binoculars.

Stavatesky struck a Napoleonic pose and peered westward, following the grey slash of the freeway across the river. The road was lined on both sides by trees and ran arrow-straight for about a kilometer before suddenly his objective came into sight. He pointed.

"That is the prize we have come to steal," he said to the major. "Klein Gastrose."

The major dutifully turned his binoculars towards the German village and studied the ground carefully. The terrain was flat farm fields broken by small, neat clumps of forest that grew sprinkled on either side of the road. Some of the fields south of the village were freshly plowed.

"The land is very flat," the major sucked at his teeth and made an unhappy face. "From the moment we cross the bridge, we will be exposed to enemy fire."

General Stavatesky looked at the man like he was an idiot. "What enemy fire, you dolt?" he snapped irritably. "Do you see any sandbags, or tank traps? It is a sleepy little village on the ass-end of the battlefront. Do you think the local farmers have machine guns? We will drive straight through the center of the settlement and seize the crossroads. Then we will radio Western Army Command to send in the tanks to turn the allied flank."

"What about the villagers?" the major wanted to know.

That was an important question because it would determine the attitude of his men.

"Kill them," Stavatesky did not hesitate. "We are at war. Every German is an enemy of Russia. Shoot them dead."

He checked his watch a final time. The delays they had encountered en route had forced him to modify his plans out of necessity. It was almost midday. He could not expect armored support from Army Command before dawn the next morning. He would have to seize the village and hold it overnight before relief could be expected. It was a setback, but not a significant one. The war would still be won – just a day later than he had planned.

He set his binoculars down and gave a great sigh, like a man about to embark on a long journey, then turned one final time to survey his battle force. He had some fifty armored personnel carriers and around eight hundred men. Seizing Klein Gastrose would be a cake-walk.

"Get the APCs rolling," he declared with a dramatic flourish. "The Motherland is counting on us. We are going to war, major. Let us ride into battle like triumphant heroes. We attack immediately."

KLEIN GASTROSE, GERMANY

Chapter 3:

Purcell's evacuation instructions to the Devereaum staff had caused so much distracting consternation and chaos on the streets of Klein Gastrose that when the radio on his hip crackled to life, he was startled by the sudden squawk.

"Purcell," he snatched for the receiver and thumbed the transmit button.

"Colonel, this is Hadley. I'm with Jumbo at an OP halfway between the village and the bridge into Poland," the man on comms spoke quickly, his voice incredulous. "You're not going to believe this, sir, but the Russians are coming."

Purcell grinned dismissively for a moment, but then something troubling in Hadley's voice caused him pause.

"You're shitting me, right?"

"No, sir," Hadley's voice sounded disbelieving. "There is a column of old BTR-50s crossing the bridge as we speak, heading directly for the village."

Purcell felt his heart stop beating for a long moment of shock, and then all his senses seemed to scream an overwhelming chorus of alarm.

"Are you sure?" It made no sense. If the enemy were launching an attack, where was the massed artillery bombardment and the air cover? The Russians weren't the masters of surprise; their military *modus operandi* was characteristically brutal, blunt and deliberate.

"Colonel, I spent six years at the Fulda Gap in the '80s. I know what a fucking BTR-50 looks like."

"How many?"

"Unknown," Hadley said. "The lead vehicles are just crossing the bridge now, but judging by the sound and the diesel smoke, this is not a scouting mission. It's a full-on enemy incursion."

"Tanks?" he felt a slide of twisting fear knot his guts.

"No. Not that we can see. Just a shit load of APCs making straight towards the village," Hadley said.

"Fuck!" Purcell spat, then as an afterthought he said, "You and Jumbo get back to the trucks right now. Move it!"

For another long thumping heartbeat of dismay, Purcell stood rooted to the spot, and then suddenly he exploded into action.

The hotel was the only structure in the settlement with any kind of elevation. The two-story building had a brick and white plaster façade, criss-crossed with dark wooden beams to give it the enchanting look of decorative fachwerk.

Purcell dashed through the front door of the hotel and looked desperately around. The ground floor was given over to a restaurant and a reception area. He found a staircase against the far wall and took the steps two-at-a-time. He burst onto the upper floor corridor and ran towards the closed door at the end of the passage. The door burst back on its hinges under the weight of his boot, and he ran to the far window and ripped back the curtains.

From his vantagepoint towards the east he now had a view of the Lusatian Neisse Bridge. What he saw made him gasp and recoil in horror.

A column of Russian BTR-50s were cresting the bridge and trundling into Germany. He counted eight of the old Russian APCs, but he knew there would be more of the squat troop carriers still unseen. They were traveling slowly beneath a pall of black belching exhaust smoke; a seemingly endless procession of ugly angular grey steel heading directly towards him.

Purcell ran back along the passage and down the stairs with the radio clasped tightly in his hand, barking orders as he went.

"Tom! Tom! We've got a fucking column of Russian APCs coming towards us. They're crossing the bridge right now. Recall Bluey and get the men assembled pronto – and get the Javelins unloaded from the trucks. We're going to need them."

He reached the ground floor of the hotel and burst out through the door onto the main street of the village. He found the company's RTO standing in the shade of a sidewalk tree. The RTO was a nuggety, stockily-framed man who had served with the 101st Airborne. He had two bad knees and walked with a permanent pronounced limp, but he was ice-cold under pressure and an expert at unarmed combat. His name was Pat Devline, but his nickname was 'Sniper's Nightmare'. Purcell gestured frantically to Devline, and the retired paratrooper hobbled towards him.

"Get on the radio to anyone and everyone you can," Purcell spoke in an urgent staccato. "Find someone up the chain in the Big Army and tell them that the Russians are attacking."

"Are you for real, sir?" Devline balked.

"This ain't no drill," he assured the man. "There's a convoy of Russian APCs about a mile away, coming closer."

Devline dashed to the back of a truck to fetch his bulky radio equipment and Purcell searched the street for Hawker. He found the XO fifty paces away, behind one of the trucks, surrounded by a knot of Devils. They were unloading the weapons and ammunition. Purcell pulled Hawker aside, his face working with agitation.

"I want a platoon of men in the hotel and spread amongst this cluster of buildings armed with the four Javelins," he rattled off orders, trying to force his thoughts into logical order and knowing that every second the enemy was drawing inexorably closer. "I want the other two platoons in the buildings that line the north-south route. Understand?"

Hawker nodded.

"Where's Bluey?"

"He's just been on comms. He's a kilometer south of the town. He was finishing off his recce. He and the others will be back any minute."

"Okay," Purcell took a deep settling breath. "When he returns, I want him and the rest of the guys from the LandCruiser to work their way forward of the village on foot using the irrigation ditches that skirt the farm fields. Tell them to take a couple of M240s and find covered enfilading fire positions, but not to shoot until I give them the order. Am I clear?"

"Crystal," Hawker nodded. "I'll make it happen."

"And get these trucks hidden," Purcell added in afterthought. "Find a back alley or a side road to park them where they will be protected from enemy fire."

"Okay," Hawker jerked his head.

His instructions issued, Purcell turned round to search the street for Gary Wrexford, but Hawker seized the Colonel's arm, pulling him back.

"Frank, are we really going to try to fight these bastards off?" Tom Hawker croaked. "They're in APCs for Christ's sake and they probably outnumber us ten to one."

Frank Purcell looked grim and despairing. "We don't have a choice," he said flatly. "If we pull out now and leave this village to the Russians, every man, woman and child will be slaughtered. And the Russians will have a toehold south of the battlefront. You saw all the armor that's being rushed north towards Berlin. If the Russians take this village and can get their own tanks here quickly enough, those allied supply lines could be completely severed. We have to hold the fuckers off until we can be reinforced. I don't like it. It's suicidal. But it's our only move."

"So, we're fucked." Hawker summed up.

"Completely fubared," Purcell agreed. "Now move your ass and make something happen."

The two men broke apart and Purcell went in search of Gary Wrexford. He found the man inside the Devereaum office building, hastily stuffing documents and files into an old leather briefcase.

"The Russians are coming," Purcell had no time for diplomacy. "An armored column has just crossed the bridge. The first enemy APCs will be here within the next three or four minutes."

Wrexford looked utterly astonished. "Good Christ!" he swore, and then his face crumpled into an expression of debilitating terror. "What do we do? Where do we go?"

"We're not going anywhere," Purcell said. "We're going to fight. Your job is to get your people to the waiting trucks and keep them calm. If it looks like the Russians are going to overrun the village, I will send drivers to take you and your staff to safety. But until then, you keep everyone close to the trucks and out of harm's way. Understand?"

"Yes... yes..." Wrexford seemed numb with shock.

"And find the mayor," Purcell couldn't remember the name of the elderly German man he had been introduced to. "Let him know what is happening. Tell the locals to get as far away from here as they can, right now before the shooting starts."

*

Word of the advancing Russian column spread like wildfire. Villagers started screaming, scattering in fear. Old women dropped to their knees, paralyzed with dread and began to weep. A couple of cars sped recklessly across the road, swerving in panic and then disappeared towards the south. Mothers grabbed their children by the wrist and ran for their homes. A handful of men came out onto the street brandishing old rifles. Others tried to herd their families to safety, carrying bags of belongings, looking frantically over their shoulders for a sight of the approaching Russians. Throughout the wave of terror and mayhem, the Devil's Detail hastily went about their work.

The trucks were moved out of sight and soldiers from 1st Platoon carried the four Javelins and the reloads up onto the top story of the hotel and began to pile furniture and bedding against the windows. Some men took up positions on the rooftop of the Devereaum offices while others barricaded themselves in shops with fields of fire that could sweep the main road once the enemy came into sight.

The remaining two platoons retreated to the main street shopfronts, lugging spare ammunition and grenades with them. Some men took cover behind parked cars, others behind store fixtures like counters and overturned tables.

There was no time to prepare themselves further, no time to reinforce their positions. The panic became infectious. Tom Hawker took command of the two platoons that would defend the main north-south route and Purcell took command of the advance platoon who would be first to face the enemy. The Colonel prowled along the hotel corridor quickly checking each man's firing position and spoke quietly and calmly to the four Javelin teams, giving clear instructions.

"Only fire when you are sure of your shot," he went from team to team. "Forget about top-attack mode," he warned each crew. "Use direct-fire only. Aim for the lead vehicles and try to pile them up on the highway. I want to hit them hard and give them reason to pause. We must stop their momentum."

Bluey returned from his recce of the village outskirts and Hawker gave him his instructions. The Australian nodded, understanding what he was being asked to do immediately. He turned and barked orders to the handful of men with him as they piled out of the LandCruiser.

"Come on, you bastards!" the former SAS operative growled with a macabre kind of relish and a ghoulish grin. He snatched for an M240 and a handheld radio set and started to run towards the plowed fields beyond the eastern edge of the village. "Move your arses! It's time to earn our money."

*

General Stavatesky stood by the side of the road next to his command vehicle and watched the column of BTR-50s trundle past him as they made their advance across the bridge, into enemy territory. The APCs moved at slow speed, spaced twenty meters apart, like they were parading along the streets of Moscow. The drivers sat at their controls and peered ahead through their vehicle's center hatch, studiously watching the highway directly before them, while the commanders each stood stiffly behind their round, forward-opening cupolas, one hand resting on the mounted KPVT machine gun.

Directly behind the two crewmen, and squeezed close together, the troops being transported to war sat on hard benches that ran the full width of the vehicle, listening to the rumble from the engine compartment, the men wheezing and spluttering under a pall of diesel exhaust.

General Stavatesky snapped a salute, and the APC commanders returned the gesture as they lumbered past.

The general understood the significance of the moment; it was a solemn occasion. The Motherland was on the attack, pouring into Germany behind enemy lines. It was a scene torn from a heroic Russian propaganda film, and as he watched each vehicle pass, he felt a twinge of envy.

He had thought to lead the attack in his command vehicle; a triumphant Caesar at the head of a fighting column, his chin thrust out with arrogant contempt of the enemy, his heart welling with patriotic pride. But at the last moment he had rejected the idea as petty and unnecessary.

"Let the troops share the glory," he decided magnanimously. "Their victory does not diminish my tactical triumph."

The infantry major's vehicle rumbled past, tenth in the line of APCs. The major stood behind the vehicle commander and saluted Stavatesky.

"Make Russia proud," the General gruffed. "Our victory is assured."

The vanguard of the armored column reached the gentle arch of the bridge and disappeared from sight, crossing over into Germany. Stavatesky gave one last salute and then leaned in through the open hatch of his command vehicle.

"Driver. Start your engine and be ready to take me to the battlefront when I give the order. The Motherland is impatient for our victory."

*

Frank Purcell watched the procession of grim Russian APCs crest the hump of the bridge and trundle forward, holding his impatience in check, while the crews manning the Javelins went about the work of powering up the CLUs with quiet haste. The Javelin was a fire-and-forget man-portable anti-tank system with a 'soft launch' feature to help disguise the weapon's firing position. Those factors were important to Frank Purcell; he couldn't afford to lose one of the precious weapons to an errant burst of enemy machine gun fire.

"As soon as you shoot, you move," he got eye-to-eye with each of the Javelin crews to drive home the importance of his message. "You can't remain static. Once the battle starts, we're going to get hammered hard with Russian counter-fire. So, I want you to shoot, then find another position before you fire again. Understand?"

The crews nodded, grim-faced and growing anxious. The Russian APCs were closing quickly and with every passing moment more of the troop carriers appeared across the bridge. Purcell went back to the bedroom window and pressed his binoculars to his eyes.

He could see about fifteen of the enemy BTRs now, advancing in single file along the wide expanse of the tree-lined freeway. They were moving slowly, keeping parade-ground order. The vehicles in the vanguard of the column had closed to within seven hundred meters of the village outskirts.

"Find your targets and open fire!" Purcell gave the fateful order.

The four crews found different firing positions within the hotel. One team went up to the building's roof. Another crew pushed Purcell away from the window where he stood and took up position. Purcell dashed down the stairs and ran out onto the street, staring towards the bridge, holding his breath.

Forty long seconds elapsed, and then suddenly the highway east of Klein Gastrose erupted into a thunderstorm of roaring sound and violent explosions.

At such close range, and with strong heat signatures to lock on to, the American Javelins could hardly miss. In three shambolic, shattering seconds the vanguard of the advancing Russian column was turned into an inferno of twisted metal and leaping flames.

The BTRs were clad only in a thin veil of armor; just enough to protect the sides of the vehicle from a spray of enemy small arms fire. The Russian APCs were no match for the cataclysmic killing impact of the Javelin's HEAT missiles.

The lead APC was struck front on and exploded into a million jagged steel fragments, seemingly vaporized by the devastating force of the impact and then the subsequent roiling fireball that killed every man aboard instantaneously. The mangled remains of the vehicle disappeared behind a black plume of smoke and the second vehicle in the line rammed head-first into the carnage, the driver unable to stop in time. The crashed APC became engulfed in flames and the twelve men crammed into the troop compartment were forced to hurl themselves over the side of the vehicle to escape the searing flames.

The third BTR-50 was blown-apart a heartbeat later; torn wide open by a Javelin warhead. The missile exploded in an ear-splitting roar of sound that seemed to shake the very air and startled flocks of birds from the trees into raucous flight. The APC disintegrated into a scything hail of flung steel fragments, killing every man aboard in a savage flash of light.

The remaining two Javelins fired, scoring more hits and turning the wide expanse of the freeway into a mangled burning junkyard of Russian iron. Vast black oily clouds of smoke mushroomed into the sky and the flames spread to a nearby tree. The blacktop was effectively blocked and the trailing line of APCs were forced to grind to a halt, like they were stranded in a peak hour traffic snarl.

The Russian major commanding the two battalions of infantry stared, aghast for a long moment of astonishment, his eyes taking in the sudden devastation and slippery fear coiling in his guts. Then his training took over.

"Get out! Get out of the fucking APCs!" he reached for his radio and roared his orders, then grabbed his terrified driver by the throat and throttled him. "Don't stop, you dolt! Get off the fucking freeway. Make for the fields to our left."

Dozens of infantrymen began spilling over the sides of the stalled APCs, scattering into the plowed fields on either side of the freeway, followed by the major's BTR-50 and a handful of other vehicles that had survived the cataclysmic impact of the first shock American attack.

Frank Purcell, stood in the middle of the road and watched the Javelin attack from in front of the hotel. He saw the panicked enemy infantry bailing out of their vehicles and reached for his radio handset, a cruel twist on his lips.

The next few minutes would be critical, he knew. It took at least thirty seconds for a well-trained crew to reload and re-power a Javelin CLU. But his men would be hampered by the need to move first, changing firing positions, so as not to present themselves as a target to the enemy's machine guns. He figured that would take time – time he didn't have. He needed to maintain the element of surprise. He needed to hit the Russians again, before they recovered from the initial shock and began to organize themselves into a fighting force.

The smoke across the highway was picked up by a gentle breeze and blown southwards; carried like a drifting black curtain across the closest fields, smudging the outlines of the Russian infantry and giving them the illusion of concealment.

"Bluey? Where are you and your men?" Purcell thumbed the radio switch and listened through a hiss of static.

"I'm flat on my guts in the middle of a fucking drainage ditch, covered in horse manure and cow shit," the Australian grumbled. "We're in firing positions about five hundred meters east of the hotel and about three hundred meters from the highway."

"Can you see the Russian infantry bailing out of their troop carriers?"

"Clearly," Bluey said. "Some have gone to ground in the fields in front of us. Others are milling around, still positioned close to the highway, like they're waiting for orders."

"Kill them," Frank Purcell said softly.

"With pleasure," Bluey snarled.

The Australian had spread his handful of men in a line eastward along the field's drainage ditch, with an M240 at each end, so they were parallel to the road and had the Russians in enfilading fire. They were all lying prone in shallow cover and filthy with mud. Bluey turned and passed the order to the others.

"The boss wants the fuckers dead," the Australian said. "So don't fuck this up."

At three hundred meters range, and with the Russians standing in tight knots at the back of their APCs, huddled together like a flock of chickens, it was easy, savage work. Bluey fired first and a heartbeat later the clattering roar of the second machine gun joined the killing chorus, mowing down the Russians in droves before they could react. A dozen enemy soldiers went down in the first couple of seconds, some killed outright, others cruelly wounded. Bullets clanged off the hull of the steel troop carriers in violent sparks. One Russian was struck in the chest and slammed against the vehicle he stood beside. The impact of the hit from the M240 bowled the man over and ripped a cup-sized hole in his chest. He slid to the ground, numb and uncomprehending, blood drenching his tunic. The man beside the victim ducked instinctively and that small reflex saved his life. He threw himself to the ground and scurried beneath the APC, seeking shelter behind the vehicle's great steel tracks.

"Keep hitting the Russian fuckers!" Bluey snarled. He was firing in short bursts but struggling to restrain himself. "Mow them down!"

The veteran operating the second M240 had a cooler head and the detached mindset of a sniper. He picked off a group of men cowering behind a stalled BTR with the callous, clinical precision of a surgeon, tearing the knot of men to shreds in a few short seconds. Blood streaked the sides of the lead Russian troop carriers and splashed in puddles on the blacktop.

Some of the exposed Russian infantry simply threw down their weapons and ran back towards the bridge, trying to hide themselves amongst the drifting wall of smoke. Others quickly scurried to the far side of the vehicles where they were protected as bullets whanged off metal all around them. A few men in an APC who had not dismounted their vehicle began counter-fire from their troop compartment, propping their AK-74 assault rifles over the rim of the upper steel ledge and shooting into the distance.

The enemy troops who had thrown themselves down in the fields fared better than the men who had been caught standing close to their vehicles. They had been lying in the furrowed dirt, facing the village, but when the enfilading fire began, they quickly realized they had been caught in the flank by the enemy. They wriggled on their stomachs to confront the new threat and opened fire, shooting wildly.

A Russian bullet thudded into the mud close to Bluey's head and he growled his outrage.

"The bastards!" he sounded affronted, and squeezed the machine gun's trigger again, changing aim to a small group of Russians who were running for their lives. He caught one man in the legs and the soldier fell in a screaming heap, writhing on the ground in agony, clutching for his thigh. His comrade stopped, reached a helping hand out to the victim, and was shot in the face for his gallantry. The brutal impact of the bullet strike shattered the man's skull and turned the remains of his head to a custard-colored pulp that was dashed against the steel hull of an APC. He was dead before his body hit the ground.

Belatedly, some of the crews of the stalled, stranded BTRs popped off smoke canisters, adding to the swirling grey-white veil of confusion until it seemed as if the entire Russian column all the way back to the bridge had been shrouded.

Bluey and his men continued to fire, regardless, still getting some hits but more importantly adding to the hysteria that had enveloped the Russian convoy.

Frank Purcell had watched the gruesome slaughter from the outskirts of the village and nodded grim satisfaction. The Russian advance had been stalled and the infantry were cowering for cover or fleeing back towards the bridge. He held the radio to his mouth and barked an order to Bluey.

"That's it! That's enough. You guys have done your job, now get the hell back here as quick as you can."

Bluey acknowledged the order, but still delayed long enough to fire one last long burst of bullets at the enemy, emptying the machine gun's belt and causing more chaos.

"We're out of here," he passed the word to the others. "Keep you fucking heads down and start crawling back towards the village."

The sudden fraught silence following the aftermath of Bluey's surprise attack became filled with Russian voices; some men screaming, some men shouting. The Russian major commanding the infantry was trying desperately to regain some level of control, pushing and shoving men into ranks and gesturing wildly at the drivers of the stalled BTRs. The entire advance had ground to an ignominious halt and until order could be restored, the major knew how vulnerable his troops were.

"Get those fucking vehicles off the road!" he ran down the column of parked troop transports. "Get them into the fields. Fan out and start laying down covering fire with the machine guns. Clear the road! Clear the road!"

More than half his force of BTRs were still on the Polish side of the bridge, and until he could re-establish order amidst the death and mayhem, the fight for the village would be stalled. He needed to clear the bridge in order to bring the rest of the column's APCs into the fight.

"Spread out! Spread out!" the major ran down the line of stalled APCs, screaming orders. Another handful of BTRs pulled off the freeway and jounced into the surrounding farm fields, popping off smoke. The vehicle commanders crouched behind the mounted heavy machine guns and began firing wildly towards the village.

Panicked suppressing fire ripped through the streets of the hamlet, punching holes in roofs, walls and windows. An abandoned car caught fire and one of the buildings along the main street began to burn. The premises was a small fashion boutique, defended by three of the Devils. They evacuated the building before the flames caught hold, and ran crouched to find new cover.

Frank Purcell flung himself down into cover behind a low brick wall just as Russian machine gun fire began to flail the village. He landed hard, face-down on the sidewalk, and felt the air around him turn hot as bullets sprayed the wall protecting him and gouged chunks of stone from the masonry. The sound of the fusillade that ripped along the wide street was like a storm in full fury, whiplashing the air with death.

The Russian counter-fire seemed to go on forever; a relentless tempest of fury that made movement along the street and inside the buildings almost impossible. All the Devils could do was hunker down and stay in hard cover until the roar of fire finally abated.

When Purcell dared to steal a furtive glance back towards the river, he saw eight Russian BTRs spread out across the farm field adjacent to the highway, moving forward through a drifting veil of black smoke. The vehicles were advancing on the hamlet, but proceeding with wary caution. Behind them, sheltered behind their hulking steel shapes, were perhaps a hundred or more Russian infantry, following the tracks. Purcell glanced left. The freeway was still jammed with the burning mangled carcasses of the destroyed APCs and littered with dead bodies, followed by a traffic jam of more stalled APCs that reached all the way back to the crest of the bridge. Some of those vehicles were trying to get off the road and into the fields, but others were simply halted and unmoving.

Then one of the BTRs advancing across the field popped off smoke and another white wall of haze began spreading ahead of the hamlet. On cue, the Russian heavy machine guns mounted aboard the APCs began firing once more, laying down a wall of savage firepower to suppress enemy resistance as they closed inexorably.

For a moment Purcell felt utterly helpless – and then a flash of flame fizzed along the length of the street on a wavering tail of grey smoke.

The Javelin had been fired from a building on the opposite side of the wide road from where Purcell was crouched. It dashed eastward like a loosed arrow and struck one of the BTR-50s in the center of the advancing line. The Russian APC exploded to pieces and the air seemed to shudder with the killing force of the impact. Shrapnel chunks were flung a hundred yards into the air like jagged knives. An orange fireball engulfed the front end of the vehicle for a split second of inferno-like heat, and then a black billowing cloud of smoke began to rise into the sky.

The APC disappeared; obliterated in a savage second of unholy violence. The blast killed every man aboard the vehicle instantaneously and knocked down the men trailing in the APC's wake, killing a handful outright and maiming the others.

The shock and awe of the Javelin strike plunged the rest of the advancing Russian vehicles into wild panic. Three of the BTRs impulsively accelerated and charged towards the hamlet at high speed, their engines howling as they veered from side to side, weaving erratically to throw off enemy fire. But the other four APCs all braked to a violent halt and then began turning back towards the freeway, hell-bent on retreating out of enemy range.

The major leading the make-shift attack was mounted in the troop compartment of the advancing APC closest to the road. The instant after the explosion his vehicle's driver slammed to a halt. The major rose from his bench, appalled, and shouting.

"Keep going forward you dolt!" he screamed above the noise of the vehicle's clunking engine. "Attack! Attack!"

The driver dutifully obeyed and the BTR lunged forward again, but the rest of the line had descended into chaos. The four retreating APCs turned quickly back towards the road, offering themselves as broadside targets to the Javelins and the suppressing machine gun fire that had covered the advance began to falter, giving the Devil's Detail a much-needed moment of respite.

The Javelin crews crept from cover and picked their targets. The closest of the charging APCs was less than five hundred yards from the outskirts of the hamlet, swerving drunkenly from side to side across the fields like a downhill skier on a snow slope, leaving the hapless dismounted infantry in their wake stranded and cruelly exposed. The two BTRs in the middle of the line were both targeted in 'direct attack' mode, and both destroyed in quick succession.

The dual explosions were like savage thunderclaps that shook the air and echoed across the clouds. The lead BTR was torn wide open by the impact of the Javelin missile and reduced to twisted scrap metal in a single searing second of violence. The warhead aboard the missile wrenched the front end of the vehicle into a mangled ruin, killing both crewmen and consuming the shattered hulk in a blinding flash of fireball. Black smoke spewed into the sky to mark the vehicle's death, burning fiercely as an oil fire. A handful of Russian infantry trailing the APC were cut down by shrapnel. One man screamed out in pain; his tunic splashed in blood. A junior officer folded quietly forward clutching his guts and fell to the ground without a sound. He fell into the dirt and lay like a sleeping man while those around him who had also been struck by shrapnel moaned and cursed fate's cruelty as their lives bled away.

There was a single terror-filled heartbeat of pause between the first BTR explosion and the second. It was just enough time for the drivers of the remaining Russian personnel carriers to realize their own danger; just enough time for the poor bloody infantrymen following the advance to witness their comrades being mercilessly flensed by shrapnel. Then the surviving vehicle in the middle of the line was struck and obliterated. In the blink of an eye the fifteen-tonne steel troop transport was reduced to twisted debris, hurled onto its side by the explosive impact of the missile strike and engulfed by flames. Another fireball climbed into the sky but then almost immediately seemed to be suffocated by a tower of black smoke. A hail of steel fragments slashed through the air, deflecting wickedly off the sides of the surrounding APCs and cutting down more infantry who had been caught in the blast zone. A Russian sergeant sagged to his knees, clutching at his throat, his eyes bulging with astonishment as pain overwhelmed him and three nearby infantrymen all suffered minor wounds. Those men who had miraculously avoided injury stared at each other for an incredulous moment of relief – and then turned and fled back towards the freeway.

In the aftermath of the dual explosions, Frank Purcell rose cautiously from cover and peered towards the tree-lined fringe of the river. He saw the two newly-destroyed BTRs through the clouds of smoke and nodded with grim satisfaction. The rest of the surviving enemy APCs were retreating back towards the freeway with the Russian infantry blundering behind them. Purcell snatched for his radio and got on comms to the platoon lieutenant who was commanding his men from somewhere inside the hotel.

"I want machine gun fire!" Purcell barked. "Hit those bastards before they can reach the safety of cover. Cut them down."

An M240 machine gun opened up from a hotel's rooftop, filling the air around the retreating Russian infantry with a new lethal threat. Bullets scythed the open field, cutting down more enemy troops. Two men fell into the dirt clutching leg wounds, writhing in pain as white-hot lances of agony wrenched screams from their throats. Others simply dropped dead, killed instantly. One lieutenant took a flurry of rounds in the chest as he turned to scream at his men. A young rifleman, fresh-faced and new to the war, died on his back in a puddle of his own urine, his stomach ripped open and the bulging contents of his guts in his lap. The others ran on, terror snapping at their heels, blundering across the uneven plowed ground. Some men swore and screamed in panic. Some mouthed silent prayers for salvation. Others bargained with their god for survival, vowing to mend their evil ways or become benevolent if they survived the ordeal. For many, their prayers fell on deaf ears, as death hunted them remorselessly.

A knot of retreating Russian troops were all cut to pieces in two brutal seconds; slaughtered before they could reach the edge of the road. Five men went down in the same savage instant, knocked off their feet with sickening wounds. A couple died instantly but the others spent their last tortured moments in gruesome pain, abandoned by their comrades who were hell-bent only on their own survival.

The Russian major leading the attack stared aghast at the devastation and smoking ruins from his command vehicle, then snarled an order at his driver to stop. Of the eight vehicles that had commenced the advance across the field only five had survived. Perhaps as many as forty infantrymen were either dead or wounded.

"Turn us around. Get us back to the freeway," the major barked, the bitter humiliation of defeat like shards of broken glass in his mouth. He cut across the radio network, seething with indignation and made it clear to each vehicle commander that their incompetence had collectively failed him, and Mother Russia.

"Fall back across the river immediately. All vehicles will fall back across the river," he clutched the radio handset in his fist like he was strangling it. "None of you are fit to serve your country. You have brought shame upon yourselves and the glorious reputation of the army."

The crewmen waiting fretfully in the stranded line of vehicles still strewn along the freeway welcomed the order with enthusiastic relief, oblivious to the abuse of their officer. The vanguard of the column had been smashed to pieces by enemy anti-tank fire and they had no desire to put their own lives at pointless risk. Quickly, the Russian APCs began to swing across the blacktop, some making awkward three-point turns, others veering off the edge of the road in order to reverse their direction. Dozens of mounted infantry who had watched the attack from their vantage points inside the waiting APCs that were queued atop the bridge impulsively leaped from their transport vehicles and retreated on foot until the entire length of blacktop became chaotically jammed with running men and retreating APCs, everyone hastened by the hysteria of their fear.

The major's command vehicle was the last BTR on the road, its ancient engine bellowing and belching diesel exhaust as it fled the debacle, accelerating to catch up with the retreat, its three whip antennas swaying like tree branches in a gale. The major stood in the open-topped troop compartment and turned back towards the hamlet, looking for an inbound tell-tale streak of grey smoke that would signal his imminent death – but he saw nothing.

It was perhaps a pity, he thought, anticipating the wrath of General Stavatesky.

Death might have been kinder than facing the consequences of ignominious retreat.

Chapter 4:

General Stavatesky had personally witnessed the failed fiasco from the apex of the bridge, his ruddy features wrenched into an expression of monstrous disbelief.

He had been impelled from the snug sanctuary of his command vehicle by the first violent explosion, numb with unforeseen shock, so that for the first few seconds he could scarcely credit his ears. Then the second explosion had sounded and with a sick slide of despair, Stavatesky had realized the tiny hamlet of Klein Gastrose had been defended by the enemy.

He had run, sweating and laboring to the crest of the bridge and stood, numb-struck with dismay, binoculars in hand and surrounded by a six-man security detail. He pressed the binoculars to his eyes, though they were hardly necessary; the devastation was plain to see.

The first few BTRs in the vanguard of the column were burning, blackening wrecks, their twisted carcasses slewed and mangled across the highway, and the verges of the tarmac were littered with dead bodies. Behind them the procession of following APCs was backed up all the way to the Polish side of the bridge, the vehicle engines idling and the commanders helpless with confusion.

Stavatesky felt somehow betrayed. He had expected the German hamlet to be populated by a few hundred scared civilians who would run, fleeing for their lives – not defended by allied infantry units.

He turned red-faced with rage to his security team and roared at them in a fit of unholy fury.

"Turn these fucking vehicles around and get them off the bridge!" his face mottled with temper. He waved his arm at the stalled line of BTRs like a petulant child in a fit of tantrum. "Clear the road!" Until the route was cleared, the halted vehicles on the German side of the bridge were easy targets for enemy fire.

The security team ran from vehicle to vehicle, snapping instructions to the waiting commanders until, one-by-one, the APCs began the complex process of reversing or turning.

His orders issued, Stavatesky focused his attention back to the far side of the bridge to watch the fight for the hamlet unfold. A handful of BTR-50s had managed to extricate themselves from the traffic jam and spill into the farm fields south of the road. He counted eight vehicles, fanning out and forming a line. Some of the troops dismounted their transports to follow the attack, but they came under enemy machine gun fire from the flank and were mowed down.

"Incompetent idiots!" General Stavatesky growled.

Belatedly, a couple of BTRs fired smoke canisters, shrouding the field in a drifting cloud of mist. Beneath that curtain of haze, the armored attack went in with machine guns blazing.

The assault was over almost before it began. In quick, appalling succession three of the advancing BTRs were destroyed by enemy anti-tank missile fire. The remaining vehicles abandoned their attack and retreated.

Stavatesky watched the humiliating debacle with a lump of indignation choking in his throat. He remained standing at the crest of the bridge until the BTR commanded by the infantry major had crossed back onto Polish soil. The BTR was scarred and blackened, its tracks thick with mud, its hull splashed with rivulets of blood. Stavatesky glared up at the major as the vehicle crested the bridge and the two Russian officers locked eyes. The infantry major saw the murderous glare in his general's gaze and felt an icy cold frisson of fear chill his blood.

In the Russian army, failure had dire consequences, and defeat required the slaughtered sacrifice of a scapegoat.

*

The Russian personnel carriers were strewn haphazardly throughout the grassy fields on the Polish side of the border, stretching as far back down the freeway to the abandoned border crossing point. Some vehicles were being repaired by their crews. Some were spattered in blood and caked in mud. Several had parked on the verge of the road awaiting refueling.

Around the vehicles sat the infantry, hunched and sullen and miserable in small clusters. A handful of wounded men were being attended to by medics, but most simply slept in the afternoon sun or smoked cigarettes because there was no food.

General Stavatesky stomped through the fields with a face like thunder, the infantry major trailing meekly in his wake.

Everywhere the General looked he saw more tell-tale reminders of his unit's humiliation. It was written on the frightened pale faces of the infantry, and it was etched in gouged bullet scars across the steel hulls of the APCs. It was splashed in blood and guts inside the open troop compartments, and it was a sound in the air; a drone-like irritation of the men's despairing murmured voices.

"Look at them!" Stavatesky turned suddenly and confronted the major. He gestured at a knot of men who were sitting hunched in the grass with haunted eyes and round-shouldered with despondency. "All these men had an hour ago was their pride. They were warriors of the Motherland; veteran fighting men. Look what you have done to them. You have taken away their will to fight. You have robbed them of their honor."

"Me?" the infantry major looked wounded and dismayed. "How have I done this, my General?"

"By losing!" Stavatesky roared, spittle flying from his rubbery lips. "You allowed your attack on the German village to be repulsed with barely any resistance. You turned and fled, cowering from the enemy. Your assault on the hamlet was ill-considered and consequently the men have lost the will to fight."

"My General!" the major impulsively defended himself, his own face flushing red with outrage. "I planned no such attack! I only followed your orders. When I mentioned the prospect of facing the enemy you told me the village would be occupied by feeble German villagers!"

"I said no such thing!" General Stavatesky vilified the major with an outright lie and then dared the junior officer to contradict him. The major was forced to impotently swallow the bitter slander, seething with indignation. General Stavatesky went on, superior and ruthless. "You are the infantry officer leading the attack. You are the one who was responsible for the occupation of the village. You were gifted this honor, and you have disgraced yourself."

For a long moment the two men faced off, the major wrestling to restrain his temper and the General almost gloating in his absolute power. Finally, Stavatesky relented, lowering his voice. "You will retain your rank, major, but from this moment on I am taking full command of the attack. Your leadership position is untenable; the men no longer trust your ability. Instead, I am sending you south immediately."

"South?" the major swayed a little on his feet.

"Yes. You are to take your BTR along the riverbank and find another suitable fording place into Germany. Once you have found a shallow, narrow crossing point, I want you to report back to me. We must regain the element of surprise. We must find a new route to outflank the enemy and overrun the village. Klein Gastrose must be seized before nightfall. You have one hour to complete your new task and report back to me."

The major balked, left numb by the cruel injustice of his situation. "The enemy force can be no larger than company-sized, if that many. We might only be facing a couple of platoons. If we simply called in an air-strike, or requested artillery support, we –" he began to plaintively protest, but the General abruptly cut him off, snarling.

"Fool! If we announce our attack using traditional tactics, the enemy will quickly know our intentions and respond in overwhelming force. No. We must fight this battle in a new way. We must strike the enemy like lightning, unannounced and unexpectedly. We must catch them off-balance before their commanders can reinforce."

"But General –"

"Enough!" Stavatesky narrowed his eyes and took a menacing step closer to the other man. His voice dropped to a dangerous whisper. "Go now, major. Get out of my sight and carry out your orders immediately, or else I'll have you backed up against a fucking wall and executed."

*

Frank Purcell stood in the middle of the road and watched the Russian BTRs retreat back across the Lusatian Neisse Bridge with a sense of astonishment and relief. Russian heavy machine gun fire had turned the outlying buildings of the hamlet into a war zone. One of the nearby shopfronts was still burning and the façades of several others were pock-marked with bullet strikes. An abandoned car parked on the far side of the road had burned out and now sat blackened and smoldering on melted tires in a haze of drifting smoke.

Purcell peered east and scanned the plowed fields where the hulking ruins of the destroyed Russian APCs lay. They were black ugly silhouettes against the afternoon sky, some still lit with flickering flames. Scattered in the dirt between the hulks were dozens of dead Russian soldiers. The line of carnage stretched to the freeway and told the story of the savage battle. He counted a half-dozen destroyed APCs and nodded with grim satisfaction.

In the eerie aftermath of the furor, the Devils slowly emerged from the village's buildings to inspect the damage. A couple of the men had minor wounds. One had been struck by a ricochet bullet that had severed the tip of a finger. Another had facial lacerations from flying masonry fragments.

Tom Hawker came and stood beside Purcell; the middle-aged black man's handsome face creased with a scowl. He surveyed the ruins in silence for a long moment, then licked his lips, choosing his words with careful consideration.

"Frank, we can't hold this place against an armored Russian column. If they make a determined attack, we'll be overrun."

"Agreed," Purcell conceded gravely. "But we're going to do it anyhow."

Hawker blanched. "Frank, that's crazy thinking, man. We were lucky we caught the Russians by surprise. They weren't prepared for enemy fire. Next time they will be. Next time they attack, it will be in numbers. They're not going to just drive blindly onto our Javelins again. They'll hammer us with arty first and they'll come in overwhelming numbers. We won't stand a chance."

Purcell nodded, but his expression remained stoically determined. "I'm not arguing with you, Tom. You're right. But we don't have a choice. We have to hold this place until the civilians can all be evacuated – and until our position can be reinforced by the Big Army."

Hawker looked sick and pained. "Frank, this hamlet isn't worth dying for."

"No building is worth dying for," Purcell agreed. "But strategically this village becomes the lock to an open gate. If the Russians capture it, and if they have armor waiting somewhere just over that bridge, they could drive westward and cut off our armies to the north. They're trying to turn our flank, Tom. We can't let that happen."

He turned on his heel and strode back down the street towards the intersection, passing through the ranks of milling Devils that lined the sidewalks, his eyes scanning, surveying. Most of the village's buildings were solidly constructed, despite their quaint aesthetics. The shops and homes were all nested close together. Some blocks of storefronts shared a dividing wall, other buildings were separated by narrow cobblestoned laneways. Beyond the main strip, the houses he could see were either stone or half-timbered dwellings built around a tight maze of alleys, many with street-corner cafes.

After several minutes of seemingly aimless wandering, came back to where Hawker stood, his mind made up.

"We're digging in," he declared. "And we are defending this hamlet until all the Devereaum people and the town's civilian population are evacuated to safety."

"Do we have time to prepare defenses?" Hawker sounded doubtful. "The Russians are going to attack again. They could be moving into position even as we speak."

"We'll have to make time," Purcell said.

He turned and addressed the assembled Devil's Detail, raising his voice so that his words carried to every man.

"Men, we're making a stand," he put confidence and resolve into his voice, his eyes moving from face to face, measuring the impact of his words on his troops. "This is a fight we don't want and didn't ask for – but it's a battle we can't avoid. If we fall back now, we abandon the village civilians to the brutal punishment of the Russians, and we gift the enemy a strategic point from which they could threaten the flank of the allied army defending the German border. The Russians are here for a purpose, and that's reason enough to deny them the village. If they want it, they're going to have to fight us for it."

"Sir, we're not regular army," a timid voice protested from somewhere within the ranks of the Devils. "We're FOGS, and we're unsupported."

Purcell smiled, but it was a bleak wintry expression; an almost chilling twist of his lips.

"No, we're not regular army," he acknowledged. "We're middle-aged veterans. We're not the fittest, and we're not the fastest. But we're still made of the right stuff. We're soldiers, and between us we have two thousand years of fighting experience. This might be our last chance as men to prove to the world that we're still worthy of being called warriors. And if this is where we die, then we'll die an honorable soldier's death – and I'd rather go out like a boss, than wither away in a rocking chair nursing regrets."

The Devils stirred, like stalks of wheat swayed by a gentle breeze. It had been a powerful speech that had struck a chord in all of them. It pricked at their honor and their self-esteem. It reminded them of the men they had been in their enlisted days and why they had first been inspired to take up the call to serve their country. It reawakened the heroic warrior within them.

Someone cheered impulsively, and that voice was joined by a handful of others, until all the Devil's Detail were cheering. Frank Purcell grinned wolfishly at the closest men and shouted above the sudden clamor of voices.

"Let's give the Russians the fight of their lives. I want them to forever regret the day they tangled with the Devil's Detail!"

The cheering swelled and Purcell seized on the enthusiasm and turned it to action. "Now let's get to work! We need to make the Russians pay a bloody price for every inch of ground they try to take."

*

The Devils set about reinforcing every doorway and window in the village with piled furniture and loose bedding. Fields of fire were cleared along the sidewalks by removing wastebins, bench seats and signs. Everything was thrown across the freeway to form an obstacle that might delay the advance of the Russians. Purcell and Hawker supervised the work, personally inspecting firing positions and sighting the M240 machine guns.

Homes and shops were raided for food and water, some of which was stacked aboard the heavy trucks that would carry the civilians to safety.

In the midst of the frantic work, Purcell sent a scout forward to the riverbank to get eyes on the Russians, then sought out Bluey and drew him aside. The tall brawny Australian was working with a shovel to dig a shallow firing pit next to a roadside tree, his sleeves rolled up to his elbows and his tunic soaked in sweat.

"What did you discover when you recce'd the village outskirts?" Purcell asked. It was the first opportunity the two men had to speak since the Russians had launched their sudden attack. The Australian leaned on the handle of his shovel and thought for a moment, recalling the terrain he had seen from the window of the LandCruiser.

"The ground is just continuous farm fields along the riverbank for at least five miles south of our position," he said. "That's as far past the village as I went. Beyond that, I can't say," he shrugged. "The only place of any tactical note is about three clicks down the road where the highway passes through the saddle of a low rocky ridge."

"An ambush point?"

The Aussie shrugged his shoulders and blinked sweat from his eyes. "Sure," he said. "If you could block the road, the enemy would have to detour several miles westward, or hug the banks of the river to advance. It might be a place to hold up an attack – if you're expecting one."

Purcell smiled thinly. "I don't know what to expect," he confessed. "I've thrown the scouting report I had on the Russians out the window. Everything about the enemy attack was out of left field. No artillery, no air-strike, no combined arms assault," he shook his head, mystified. "So right now, I have to believe our Russian foes are capable of anything and everything."

Bluey grunted. "You would need a Javelin and reloads, and an M240 – and a handful of men," the Aussie applied his mind to the problem of an ambush. "Can you afford to lose that much firepower from the defense of the village on the chance that the enemy might try to sweep behind our flank?"

"I can't afford *not* to take the risk," Purcell said grimly.

Bluey shrugged and reached into his pocket for a crumpled pack of cigarettes. He lit one, inhaled deeply, and turned to stare at the bridge in the distance, as if at any moment he expected to see the Russians renew their attack.

"You want me to hold the ridge?"

"Yes. Take one of the LandCruisers and the guys who went on the scouting recce with you – and a radio. Keep the line hot. I need you to protect our back. If the Russians approach in strength and it looks like you're going to be overwhelmed, get word to me."

"Okay," Bluey nodded.

Purcell gave a final grim warning. "If the Russians do try to get behind us, and if they happen to get past you, we're all dead."

*

The Devils worked to transform the tiny hamlet into a defensible position with the tireless energy of men who knew their lives were on the line. Firing loopholes were cut into walls and the barricade of rubble across the highway grew higher and wider. With the passage of every frantic minute more panic-stricken Devereaum personnel and townsfolk returned to the village center from their homes, carrying whatever personal keepsakes they could cram into a small suitcase.

Purcell and Hawker stood by the closest MAN KAT-1 and watched the first evacuees clamber aboard. The truck had been reversed up against a waist-high retaining wall to make loading the civilians into the flatbed easier. Two Devils, standing aboard the rear tray, hauled the waiting women and children up into the truck until the vehicle was fully loaded.

"Head south and then west towards Leipzig," Purcell instructed the driver. He was a Frenchman from 3rd Platoon who had once served in the Arme blindée et cavalerie as a Leclerc MBT driver. He had seen action in Lebanon and Bosnia as part of the 5e Régiment de Dragons. He had a dark swarthy face, quick restless eyes, and spoke around a cigarette dangling from the corner of his mouth.

"*Oui, je comprends,*" he shrugged his shoulders with a disgruntled Gallic, '*Bof*' to suggest he could care less about his task. He wanted to kill Russians, not drive a truck load of refugees to safety.

The KAT-1 pulled away slowly, its big engine rumbling. Purcell and Hawker watched it disappear around a bend in the road, although the sound of the truck working up through the gears lingered as an echo for several more seconds before finally fading.

In the eerie silent aftermath, Hawker turned to Purcell, the XO's face creased with concern.

"Frank," Hawker said softly. "I'm too old for this shit," he deadpanned the line from a Hollywood blockbuster film.

Purcell chuckled, despite their circumstances, and then realized Hawker was not joking. His own face became serious and thoughtful.

"Tom, you and I are like old warhorses," he spoke carefully, tapping into a lifetime of wisdom and experience. He searched for an analogy, thought of one, and went on. "During the Napoleonic wars, the cavalry were often called upon to charge the enemy's infantry lines. We're talking sometimes of thousands of horsemen in tight ranks and ornate uniforms. They would form up then move into a trot, a canter and finally a full-blown charge, their swords or lances in the air as they thundered across the ground.

"Waiting for them would be the enemy infantry, often supported by artillery. The cannons would fire and inevitably shrapnel would kill some of the cavalry. Men were knocked off their horses, thrown down to the ground – *and yet their horses would run on, keeping their place in the formation, matching the other horses stride for stride until the moment they charged – because it was the only thing those horses knew to do. They had been trained for war; it was their purpose in life.*"

Hawker looked bewildered. "Is there a point to your story?"

"We're like those riderless horses," Purcell said. "We've been highly trained, and we've developed a certain set of skills. Throughout our lives, being soldiers was the thing we did that always mattered most; that made the most difference to the world. Soldiering has been drilled into us. So, you can say you're too old for this, but there's nothing else you're more qualified to do. Fighting is instinctive to us. It's how we've been conditioned. Professional soldiers are a special breed of men. It's not just what we do, it's who we are; who we will always be… whether we like it or not."

Purcell might have said more but a sudden squawk of radio static caught his attention. He snatched for the handset clipped to his belt.

"Purcell," he acknowledged.

"Sir, it's G-Spot," a voice whispered. "We've got shit happening."

The expression on Frank Purcell's face tightened. "SITREP."

G-Spot was the nickname of the soldier Purcell had sent forward to the riverbank to scout the enemy. His real name was Chris Oliver, a former US Army grunt from 1st Platoon who had served in Afghanistan twenty years earlier. He had been nicknamed G-Spot by the Devils because they joked that he could never be located whenever there was action.

"I'm five hundred yards downstream of the bridge," G-Spot's voice through the radio was hoarse with tension and barely more than a waver of drifting static in Purcell's ear. "I'm concealed in trees and scrub on the verge of the riverbank, and I've got eyes on the enemy. The Ruskies are up to something. There's a lot of vehicle movement. It could be they're forming up for another attack."

"How many BTRs?" Purcell needed to know.

"I count thirty, but there might be more," G-Spot muttered in a stage whispered voice.

"MBTs?"

"None that I can see."

"Men?"

"Battalion strength at least," G-Spot said. "Call it six or seven hundred men. They're re-mounting their rides. Looks like they mean business."

"Okay," Purcell drew a deep breath and flashed a glance at Hawker's troubled face, thinking fast. "Get back to the village and double-time it."

"Roger that," G-Spot sounded relieved. Some of the tension went out of his voice. "I'm exfiltrating back to the village. Out."

Purcell ended the comms call and gave Hawker a more meaningful look. "G-Spot says the Russian infantry are mounting up. They might be getting ready to launch another attack. At least thirty APCs and a battalion of mech boys – maybe more."

"We're not ready," Hawker felt a flush of sudden alarm. "We need more time."

"It seems like we've had all the time we're going to get," Purcell gruffed with resigned acceptance, then his tone turned brusque and business-like. "Alert the men. I want everyone in position and ready for the fight of their lives."

*

"What's the plan?" Tom Hawker and Frank Purcell stood shoulder to shoulder at a second-floor window of the village hotel. Purcell had binoculars pressed to his eyes, peering intently towards the distant bridge, scanning the afternoon skyline for tell-tale blooms of black diesel exhaust that would herald the Russian attack.

Purcell lowered his glasses for a moment. "Two of the Javelins are forward of the village, dug in on either side of the freeway in good cover," the Colonel explained. "As soon as the first Russian BTR shows itself on the bridge, they have orders to fire and keep firing until they run out of re-loads."

Hawker nodded.

The Devils had been taken completely by surprise by the first Russian attack and as a result, the enemy had been able to get more than a dozen APCs across the bridge and into the surrounding fields. With some luck, that might have been enough to overwhelm the village. Purcell had no intention of allowing the enemy another opportunity. This time the Devils would be ready.

"If we can block the bridge and kill everything that moves, the Russians will be forced to try a river crossing," he said.

The Russian BTR-50s were Soviet-era tracked amphibious armored personnel carriers that had been based on the chassis of the old PT-76 light tank. Its flat, boat-shaped hull made it capable of crossing shallow water obstacles at low speeds.

"That will buy us some more time. Those old BTRs are slow, and not suitable to deep fast-flowing water. If we can hit them hard enough, they'll be forced to search for another way across the river. Hopefully by then we will have been reinforced."

Hawker nodded. As far as plans go, it was simple and solid.

"The third Javelin team will stay with the two platoons under your command to defend the main intersection if the Russians somehow break through our lines. Bluey has the fourth Javelin. I've sent him three miles to the south with a handful of men to defend a ridge in case the enemy try to sweep around behind us."

"You're taking a big risk, Frank. Splitting our forces..." Hawker frowned sharply.

"Yes, but we don't have a choice. We'll have to make up the shortfall in weaponry with improvised homemade bombs."

"Homemade?"

Purcell shrugged. "Molotov cocktails and maybe even ANFO bombs if we get the chance."

Molotov cocktails had been the weapon of choice for resistance fighters across Europe groups since the 1950s and had been in use since the outbreak of WW2. Typically, they were made from glass bottles filled with gasoline and secured with a cloth wick. Once the weapon was thrown and struck a target, the glass shattered, and the fuel ignited. ANFO bombs were a crude combination of common farming materials such as ammonium nitrate fertilizer, a can of hydraulic fluid, and a grenade. They were commonly packed into tight spaces to collapse a section of road, or to even bring down a building. Similar ingredients had been used in several notorious terrorist attacks, including the 1993 World Trade Center bombing.

"Do we have time?"

"We'll have to make the time," Purcell said. "We can start on the Molotov cocktails immediately."

A burst of bellowed abuse coming from a room down the hallway cut abruptly across the conversation, choking off anything else Purcell might have said. Both officers stared dumbfounded at each other while the shouting rose to a fervent pitch that verged on the edge of hysteria.

"What the fuck...?" Purcell went storming down the corridor.

He strode into a corner room and found Sniper's Nightmare propped on the edge of a narrow bed, roaring foully into the handset of his radio gear. Pat Devline looked up sharply as Purcell burst into the hotel room, the RTO's face suffused red with temper, his features mottled and swollen.

"What's the problem?" Purcell demanded.

"The fucking Big Army is ignoring us!" Devline took a deep drag of a cigarette and snorted a blue cloud of smoke at the ceiling. "I can't get anyone on the fucking line who will listen to me. Every time I try to reach someone in the chain of command, they shut me down because we're a PMC."

Purcell grunted like a boxer taking a gut punch. He thought quickly. "Okay. Fuck 'em!" he growled. "Try to get through directly to Mr. Devereaum. He'll make the bastards sit up and pay attention."

"I've tried," the former paratrooper gestured with plaintive frustration. He got to his feet and paced the room, prowling the small space, his limp pronounced. "Mr. Devereaum is on a commercial flight back to New York. His plane departed Berlin two hours ago. He's uncontactable until he lands at John F. Kennedy airport," Devline glanced at his wristwatch, "in about seven hours' time."

"Shit."

For a long moment of despair, Purcell said nothing. The Devils were backed into a corner and help was not coming. He threw up his hands in frustration. "Then get back on the radio and keep trying to find someone in the Big Army who will listen. We're not going to survive this fight unless we can get reinforced before nightfall."

"We are in position on the Polish side of the river," General Stavatesky leaned close to the radio inside his BTR-80 command vehicle and nervously made his report to CINC-West, studiously avoiding to mention the first disastrous attempt to seize Klein Gastrose. "The Lusatian Neisse Bridge is under our control, and we are making preparations to advance across the border even as we speak."

"You still have not captured the hamlet?" Chief of the General Staff Army General Mikhail Timoshyn's voice down the radio line was gruff and demanding.

"No," Stavatesky felt himself cringe. "We have had several delays, but we are now preparing to commence our attack."

"You should have been triumphant by now. I have an armored column of T-90s on standby, ready to be unleashed. What kind of delays?" Timoshyn demanded.

Stavatesky balked and felt his face flush burning hot. "Our scouts have reported that the hamlet is defended by allied infantry. This has required me to exercise necessary caution."

"What are you up against?" Timoshyn fired off the question.

"It might be as much as an armored battalion," Stavatesky lied. "They might have artillery support and anti-tank missile weapons. There could be as many as five or six hundred men facing us."

"How is this possible?" CINC-West demanded. "You said the hamlet would be undefended."

The radio hissed with waves of static for a long moment before Stavatesky finally replied. "I do not know how it is possible, my General. Perhaps the allied satellites discovered our armored column and guessed our plan. Perhaps we have been betrayed by spies," he deflected. "But I assure you, my General, that we will be victorious within an hour or two. The allies defending the village will not stand."

Stavatesky could sense CINC-West's brooding discontent down the line, and he searched desperately for a way to divert the man's temper. "How does the assault on Bad Freienwalde and Wriezen proceed?"

"It's been a fucking disaster!" Timoshyn roared into his radio. "We pushed back the French infantry holding the two towns with little trouble, but the allies counter-attacked. British Challenger tanks hit us hard, and American fighter jets over the battlefield have churned our supply lines into minced met. It's been impossible to move men forward to reinforce the ground we have won. The troops holding Bad Frienwalde are now cut off and in danger of being decimated. I'm about to issue a general order for the withdrawal," Timoshyn's voice turned bitter with frustration.

Stavatesky made suitable sounds of consolation but inwardly he was relieved. With the attack in the north failing, he still had the chance to be the hero Russia so desperately needed.

All he had to do was capture Klein Gastrose.

Quickly.

*

The infantry major returned to the Polish side of the bridge looking more like a bedraggled foot soldier than a senior officer of the Russian army. His clothes were soaked wet and caked in mud, and the hull of his BTR was streaked with grime.

He dismounted the vehicle and searched the encampment for Stavatesky. He found the General inside his BTR-80 command vehicle, parked beneath a tree by the edge of the freeway. Stavatesky was in a foul mood, bristling with impatience.

"Where the fuck have you been?" the General snarled.

"Finding a way across the river, sir," the major answered with commendable restraint, though it took every ounce of his will.

"And?"

"There is a crossing point, eight kilometers to the south," the major confirmed, his features haggard, his body seeming to sag with exhaustion. "I inspected the ford myself. It is suitable for the APCs."

"You drove your vehicle to the far bank?"

"I waded across on foot, General," the major gestured at his mud-caked uniform. "The water is no more than waist deep, and the far bank is a gentle grassy slope. It is ideal for our purposes."

"Good! Good!" Stavatesky's mood brightened instantly and a cunning sparkle glinted in his eye. He thought hard for a furious frantic moment and then made his decision.

"We will split our forces. I want you to take fifteen BTRs and one hundred and fifty of our men. I will mount a demonstration crossing the bridge to keep the allies distracted. You will command the outflanking force. Get your vehicles and men across the river and attack the village from the south."

*

General Stavatesky knew his men were demoralized. He could see it in their faces; the pathetic sullen defeatism in their expressions. He felt nothing but contempt for them; they were cattle for slaughter – but they had a purpose, and he knew that for them to fight and win, they would need to be motivated.

He climbed on top of his command vehicle, using the BTR-80 like a stage and heads turned towards him in surprise.

"Brave sons of Russia," he lifted his voice, commanding the attention of the troops. "We are an hour away from a glorious triumph. Beyond that bridge," he pointed theatrically, "is immortality and fame. You all will be hailed as heroes of the Motherland once we seize the little village of Klein Gastrose." He paused for a moment, a little shocked that the men still sat lumpen and morose, despite his patriotic entreaty. He felt himself falter and then realized that patriotism was not an appeal the men would respond to. Partisanship had died on the streets of Latvia, and in the rubble and carnage of Warsaw. The men had fought and died for love of country, and now they were weary of self-sacrifice for a higher ideal. The general tried again.

"Mark my words. The maidens of Russia will offer themselves to you like adoring slaves. You will walk tall down the streets of Moscow with medals on your chests and the favors of any pretty girl yours for the taking!" the men began to stir. Some smiled. Others exchanged wolfish glances and chuckled. They no longer had any interest in the altruistic ideal of fighting for the Motherland, but the notion of adoration and willing women spreading their legs for them was the kind of base motivation they all responded to.

"But I do not expect you to wait for our return to Moscow for your just rewards," Stavatesky went on, warming to his topic. "Because there are women in the village. Dozens and dozens of gorgeous young German *Fräuleins* who are yearning for virile Russian cock. They are all yours - and so is all the food. Bakeries and shops, crammed with bread, jams and fresh meat. It's there - just over that bridge, and once we seize the settlement you can rape, pillage and plunder until your manhood is sore and your stomach is full!"

That brought an enthusiastic cheer from the troops and Stavatesky beamed down at them like some benevolent master, concealing his loathing contempt. He spread his arms wide like a stage actor or a politician on the hustings. Some of the troops got suddenly to their feet and reached for their weapons, eager to have the business done. Others laughed and joked with lewd anticipation of victory.

"Mount up!" Stavatesky ordered. "It is time to go to war!"

Chapter 5:

Frank Purcell gathered a dozen local men around him on the sidewalk outside the village *kneipe* and issued his instructions. The men were all waiting their turn to board the trucks that would spirit them away to safety in the west, but before that happened, Purcell was determined to put them to work.

The door of the village bar hung open, and the owner of the drinking establishment had a team of three brawny youngsters bringing up crates of beer bottles from the cellar. As each crate arrived outside the doorway, Purcell and his team emptied the bottles contents into the gutter and then set about making Molotov cocktails. The air turned thick with a heady mix of gasoline and alcohol fumes as the men sat hunched in the gutter, filling each bottle from plastic fuel cans and tearing at bedsheets to make the wicks.

Purcell supervised the work with one distracted eye on the convoy of waiting trucks. The second vehicle was being loaded with more evacuees; a mixture of local women and children, and female Devereaum employees. Despite his earlier stern warnings, he noticed several villagers boarding the truck carrying bundles of clothes and lugging suitcases. He strode grimly across the road and stood by the truck's tailgate.

"No!" he shook his head. *"Nein!"*

The waiting women looked up at the tall American officer white-faced with shock and terror.

"You can take nothing with you," Purcell shook his head and reached for one of the suitcases a middle-aged lady held clutched to her bosom. He prised the battered old valise from the woman's clawed fingers and threw it into the road. The suitcase sprang open revealing a modest bundle of clothing and a scatter of framed family photographs. The lady began to wail and collapsed to her knees, appealing to Purcell with a distraught, tortured expression. She blurted a torrent of German in Purcell's direction which he did not understand.

"No!" Purcell said again, and beckoned the two Devils who were standing at the tailgate of the truck, helping passengers aboard. "No one takes anything with them," he reiterated his orders. "No suitcases, no bulky belongings." He turned back to the line of women and children. "You must only take important papers and any money you have. Nothing else."

The waiting village folk broke into distressed whines of protest but Purcell stared them down defiantly, hating himself, but knowing it was necessary.

"Every suitcase, every bundle of clothing and every keepsake takes up space on the trucks that could be used to carry another person to safety," he explained to the protesting mob, his lips a pale tight line of authority. "If you would keep your possessions with you, then tell me the names of the twenty women you would leave behind for the Russians to rape and murder. Give me their names and then you must tell them to their faces that they have to be left behind so you can keep your belongings."

That brutal reality put paid to the protests. The wails faltered to a guilty whimper and some of the villagers looked suddenly shame-faced for their indulgence. The tears dried on their cheeks and the laneway turned suddenly silent.

For another full minute, Purcell stood at the head of the line, hands on his hips, staring the mob down, making eye contact with every villager and withering them with a steely look that dared further protest. The women became downcast with embarrassment and could not meet his gaze.

Tom Hawker appeared. He had been inspecting the Devil's efforts to prepare defensive positions in the buildings that lined the main intersection and had been distracted from his work by the clamor of protesting women's voices. He stood for a moment in the shadows of the sidewalk until Purcell had finished his exchange with the village women. Hawker cast his eyes over the frantic bomb-making preparations taking place on the cobblestoned alley all around him. His gaze went to the small river of beer running down the gutters and he smiled with rueful mirth.

"If Bluey ever finds out about this..." he muttered.

Purcell grunted, mentally changing focus back to the myriad of issues pressing in on him. "He'd be apoplectic," Purcell agreed. "Wasting this much beer? I'm sure there's a law against it in Australia."

Already the first Molotov cocktails were being finished and stacked into carry crates, each beer bottle three-quarters filled with gasoline and a wick dangling from the neck. Extra wads of cloth had been packed around the wicks to hold the long tapers of cloth in place, ready to be lit and thrown.

"That's some nasty guerrilla shit you've got going on here." Hawker watched the German menfolk working with quick frantic efficiency. One of the men clumsily spilled fuel across the cobblestones in his fumbling haste and berated himself for his error.

"Do you think they'll work?" Hawker asked.

"They'll work," Purcell nodded. "The problem is that for us to use them, the Russian BTRs are going to have to be at close range. And if they get close enough for the Molotov cocktails to be an effective weapon, it's going to be because we're losing the fight, and the village is in danger of being overrun."

That was a salient point. A BTR would have to close within twenty meters to present itself as a target, and the chances of the Devils surviving the lash of Russian heavy machine gun fire as the enemy APCs advanced would be minimal. By the time the Russians surged towards the buildings that lined the intersection, most likely every one of the Devils would already be dead.

Hawker said nothing. Both men looked at each other with an unspoken fatal acceptance of their inevitable end.

Their only chance of survival was to somehow hold the Russians at arm's length, or pray to be saved by allied army reinforcements.

Neither possibility seemed very likely.

*

G-Spot returned to the village lathered in sweat and on legs rubbery with fatigue. He hadn't run so far or so fast since his enlisted days in Afghanistan. The ensuing years had not been kind to him. He was a father in his forties now with haggard features and a crop of short greying hair. He wiped sweat from his brow and squinted at Purcell who intercepted him on the road outside the village hotel.

"Where do you want me?" he doubled over and propped his hands on his knees, lungs working like giant bellows.

"Are the Russians coming?"

G-Spot shook his head. "They were mounting up when I bugged out. I don't know if they were preparing to attack, or ordering a retreat. I just high-tailed it back here after my SITREP."

Purcell grunted. He looked past G-Spot and scanned the hump of the distant bridge looking for tell-tale blooms of black diesel exhaust but could see nothing.

"There are crates of Molotov cocktails being assembled in one of the laneways behind the main intersection," he turned and pointed back along the road to where he had left the German menfolk toiling in the street. "Take one other man with you and carry them forward. I want them distributed to everyone."

G-Spot beckoned another Devil and the two of them set off together towards the intersection. A crackle of garbled radio chatter made Purcell snatch for the radio on his hip.

"This is Purcell," he said quickly. "Repeat your message."

The line went dead with echo for a few fraught seconds and then a voice came down the line, unnaturally loud and frayed with tension.

"It's Brannigan and Chubby!" one of the two-man Javelin teams Purcell had positioned forward of the village on either side of the freeway reported. "The fucking Russians are coming! We can see three BTRs cresting the apex of the bridge."

Fuck!

Purcell switched onto the 1st Platoon net and issued a curt, tense warning to the men in at the hotel windows and in the nearby buildings who would be the first to engage the enemy, then spoke urgently to Tom Hawker back at the intersection.

"Tom, we're out of time, man. The Russians are attacking. There are three BTRs on the bridge and probably another twenty or thirty behind them. Get your men into position but don't open fire until the enemy reach the outskirts of the village!"

*

The thirty Russian APCs left in General Stavatesky's control formed up on the Polish side of the river and, with a throaty roar of accelerating engines, advanced towards the bridge. The vehicle commanders in the van of the column were tense and nervous, and the soldiers they were transporting who sat crammed into the open-topped troop compartments felt helpless as cattle being trucked to a slaughter yard. The soldiers had witnessed first-hand the terrible killing power of the allied anti-tank missiles during the first failed attack and now they were terrified their own death was imminent.

"Faster!" the commander leading the column of APCs demanded of his driver as the vehicle reached the hump of the bridge. From his open cupola where he stood anxiously peering ahead, he could see the little German village coming into view. The freeway beyond the bridge was still blocked with the burned-out vehicles that had been destroyed during the first attack. The BTR commander felt himself break out into a trembling sweat. "Faster!"

General Stavatesky watched the column race towards the bridge from the side of the road, leaning out through the door of his command vehicle. He reached for his radio and broadcast across the battalion net.

"The citizens of Russian hold their breath and await your glorious triumph," he launched into a stirring speech, lifting his voice above the roar of the BTR-50s as they rumbled past him. "The enemy is few and they are frightened. Kill them all. Overwhelm them with machine gun fire and write your names into the Motherland's history of immortal heroes."

It was emotive propaganda and none of the BTR commanders paid any attention. They were too tense; too fraught with their own nerve-shredded fears to be inspired by a general's sermon. Glory, immortality and patriotism were not their motivation. They only wanted to survive the coming bloodbath.

"Attack! Attack! Last time the enemy took us by surprise, but this time we are prepared. Show them how Russia's finest sons wage warfare!" Stavatesky finished his speech and threw down the radio handset so he could watch the first APCs crest the bridge, his throat dry and his heart thumping wildly in his chest. He saw the lead vehicle's commander crouched behind the personnel carrier's heavy machine gun and the moment the BTR reached the apex of the bridge and became silhouetted against the skyline, the heavy gun began firing; pouring out a torrent of lead to suppress the waiting enemy.

The real fight for Klein Gastrose had begun.

*

Purcell had positioned his two Javelin teams just beyond the outskirts of the village, about eight hundred meters from the bridge. The two-man teams were dug in on either side of the freeway, hidden and shadowed beneath trees. From where they crouched, each pair had an unobstructed view of the bridge.

Both teams had powered up their CLUs and their systems were armed and ready to shoot.

"Take the fuckers out!" Frank Purcell gave the fateful order over the radio.

Chuck 'Chubby' Washington was a fifteen-year veteran of the US Army who had seen action in the Middle East. Since finishing service with the military, he had worked as a mechanic and a farm hand for several years, restlessly drifting across the country from job to job before being recruited to the Devils at the outbreak of war. He was a steady man, unruffled under pressure.

His loader, Scott Brannigan, was an ex-Ranger who had served with the 75th Ranger Regiment and seen combat during Operation Enduring Freedom and Operation Iraqi Freedom. He was one of the youngest, fittest men in the Devils, who, despite being aged in his early forties, still wore his hair in a mohawk. A quietly-spoken loner, he was tough and utterly ruthless in a fight.

The two men heard Purcell's order over the radio and exchanged a grim meaningful glance.

"Time to go to war," Brannigan muttered.

The first Russian BTR-50 appeared as a stark squat silhouette, framed against the afternoon sky as it crested the apex of the bridge. For a weapon as lethal as the Javelin, and at such close range, it was almost a certain kill, despite the fact that the target was rattling towards them at around forty kilometers an hour. Chubby Washington hunched over the CLU and sighted the Russian APC, then squeezed the 'fire' trigger. The bulky command launch unit bucked against Chubby's shoulder and a split-second later the loaded missile flashed from the launcher on a rush of rocket propellant.

The two men watched the missile streak towards the bridge on a wavering tail of grey smoke, moving through the air like a flash of light. The missile struck the BTR-50 flush and blew the vehicle apart. A fireball enveloped the Russian APC and shards of jagged metal were flung hundreds of yards in every direction. Then a great pall of oily black smoke rose billowing into the sky. The sound of the explosion echoed like the dull distant 'crump' of an artillery shell.

The killing power of the Javelin was absolute. The BTR was all but vaporized. The ten men crammed into the troop compartment were obliterated in the searing flames.

The first time the Russians had advanced across the bridge the appalling shock and awe of the Javelins had stunned and demoralized them. This time they were manfully braced for the carnage and horror that awaited.

The following vehicle in the column swerved its path and clipped the mangled ruins of the destroyed BTR, shunting the blackened carcass sideways to the edge of the bridge and clearing a route for the rest of the column to follow.

The second BTR burst through the thick veil of smoke at twenty kilometers an hour, engine roaring as the driver crunched up through the gears. One of the trailing vehicles in the column veered out of line and shoved the burning BTR into the rail of the bridge. The wreckage plunged through space and hit the river below with a heaving splash.

"Fire!" Frank Purcell watched the Russian APCs burst purposefully through the curtain of black smoke undeterred by the first Javelin strike, the image wavering through the lenses of his binoculars. He saw the destroyed BTR freefall off the bridge and noticed charred blackened bodies of dead soldiers tumble loose from the wreckage. They hit the water and were lost from sight.

"Fire!"

The second Javelin team fired from the opposite side of the freeway, sighting on the closest BTR and unleashing their Javelin. The missile flew from the launcher in a soft 'whoosh' of noise but suddenly veered wildly in flight at the last second before impact. Thrown off course by some unknown guidance system malfunction, the Javelin climbed erratically into the sky and disappeared into the clouds.

"Missed!" Frank Purcell could barely believe his eyes. He had never seen a Javelin miss – especially one fired in 'direct-attack' mode from such close range. He stood, stunned and disbelieving for a long incredulous moment, and then felt a clammy pall of rising panic prickle the flesh along his arms.

"Christ!" he swore, and then roared into his radio. "Reload and fire! Reload!"

It would take at least thirty seconds before the Javelin teams were ready to fire again, and Purcell knew instantly that was time he didn't have. He switched frequencies on the radio and spoke urgently to Tom Hawker, waiting amongst the buildings around the intersection.

"Tom! Get your Javelin into action. Take a shot! Take a shot!"

The third and last remaining Javelin team were holed up in a single-story shopfront with a clear field of fire straight along the freeway to the distant bridge. The weapon operator hunched over his CLU and the system's seeker sought out an enemy target, locking on to the nearest BTR-50 which was now across the bridge and accelerating quickly towards the village. He flicked the 'attack-select' mode on the CLU to 'direct-attack', then made certain the unit was set to 'soft launch'. He boxed in the speeding enemy APC within the sight display and after a final moment to check everything was operational, he squeezed the 'fire' trigger.

The Javelin flew from the launch tube and Frank Purcell saw the flash and the blur of wavering smoke. He held his breath. The Javelin streaked along the freeway past the hotel where Purcell stood, rising into the air slightly and wavering before seeming to settle in flight, traveling straight and true. Purcell watched the missile all the way in until it slammed into the lead BTR and blew the vehicle to smithereens.

The impact of the strike seemed to punch the chassis of the BTR-50 backwards. The air shuddered and then the enemy troop transport was swallowed up by bright orange flame. The sound of the explosion hammered violently against Purcell's ears as the flames were overwhelmed by a rising pall of black smoke. He didn't hear the screams of the men who died. He didn't see their bodies torn to pieces or immolated by the fierce inferno. All he saw was a hailstorm of jagged debris that were heaved spinning into the air as the enemy APC was torn into a million tiny pieces of mangled steel.

"Hit the fuckers again!" Purcell growled into the radio. "Reload and keep firing!"

Already a dozen Russian APCs were across the bridge. A handful of those enemy vehicles steered straight down the freeway, heading towards the ruined BTR-50s that had been destroyed in the first Russian attack. The rest spilled into the farm fields beyond the village and began to advance. Purcell sensed already the enemy had enough men and firepower to overwhelm his position.

"Fire!" he bawled into the radio.

Chubby Washington fired a second Javelin, targeting another BTR-50 that was just cresting the apex of the bridge. The BTR-50s already in the fields and rumbling down the freeway were now simply too close for the Javelins to be effective. The official minimum range of the system was sixty-five meters but Chubby had a sneaking suspicion that the closer the range, the less likely the chance the warhead would activate before impact. There was no evidence to support his superstitious beliefs, but this wasn't the time to test the theory. Better to get a certain kill at a safe range than risk a malfunction.

He launched through a rising wall of drifting smoke and the missile flew unerringly along its path, wavering slightly in flight on its fins. It struck a Russian BTR-50 just as it began accelerating down the humped back of the bridge and blew it to pieces.

The battlefield had become a chaos of noise and thickening smoke. Three ruined enemy APCs were burning and the vehicles that were already across the bridge and had survived the initial onslaught were now popping off white smoke to camouflage their advance. The noise rose; the revving of diesel engines and the echoing boom of explosions. Then the Russian heavy machine guns mounted aboard the APCs began to lay down a wall of withering fire.

Chubby's hit on the APC was enough to temporarily block the bridge. That was a small blessing, Purcell realized. It meant that, for the moment, the dozen Russian APCs that had crossed into Germany were isolated and unsupported – but it was already a formidable force against a company of middle-aged men with just a few Javelin reloads remaining between them.

"Fire!" Purcell shouted.

The second Javelin team targeted one of the BTR-50s rattling down the road, the range decreasing with every second. The Russian personnel carrier seemed to be on a headlong collision course with the mangled ruins of the vehicles that had been destroyed in the first attack. The Javelin flew from the launcher, fired at a range of just a few hundred meters but struck one of the burned-out hulks barricading the blacktop. Frank Purcell swore bitterly. Two precious Javelins had been wasted for no reward. The odds of the Devils surviving the approaching storm blew out significantly.

"Tom!" he grabbed for his radio again.

"I'm here," Hawker acknowledged, both men shouting over the boom of explosions and the rising roar of Russian heavy machine gun fire.

"Get the second and third trucks of civilian evacuees away from the village. Pack everyone in you can and send them west before the shit hits the fan," Purcell ordered.

"Roger," Hawker acknowledged. "I'll take care of it."

The time for order and decorum had passed. Now it was simply a matter of saving as many local villagers and Devereaum personnel as possible amidst the helter-skelter chaos of a battle.

"And while you're at it, find G-Spot," Purcell thought quickly under a wall of rising pressure. "Tell him I want two crates of Molotov cocktails brought forward to the hotel, now, goddamnit. Now!"

Hawker cut comms and dashed along the street towards the line of waiting KAT-1 trucks. Purcell put the matter out of his mind. He had more pressing problems to deal with.

The heavy Russian machine guns mounted aboard each of the advancing APCs were leaving a swathe of damage, bullets thickening and heating the air with violent fury. The two-story hotel that Purcell and half of 1st Platoon were defending became an obvious landmark target for the enemy gunners. Bullets punched great holes in the masonry and brickwork walls, and shattered windows. The Devils defending the building had no choice but to hunker down and pray they would survive the dreadful maelstrom. One of the Devils was struck in the chest as he lay cowering on the floor of a second story bedroom. He was the first of the Devil's Detail to die in combat.

Purcell heard the man scream in pain and ran, crouched, down the hallway, ducking bullets. He burst into the bedroom and found the soldier on his back, his arms spread wide, his guts a mess of blood and gore. The man's haggard face was a pale mask of pain, his eyes wide and sightless. Purcell hesitated in the threshold of the doorway, aware that the man was already dead, and felt a crushing weight of despair punch the wind from his lungs. He sagged at the knees for a moment of remorse and then forced himself to stiffen. There was no time to grieve. In the next few hours many more would die; it was an inevitable tragedy of war.

He dashed back along the corridor in time to see two BTR-50s take up hull-down positions on the freeway behind the Russian APCs that had been destroyed in the first assault. Covered by the twisted wreckage, the two vehicles stopped and the soldiers they were transporting bailed out of the troop compartment and went to ground.

Purcell understood the threat immediately. From their position just a few hundred meters from the outskirts of the village, the Russian heavy machine guns and the infantry fire would be able to suppress the Devils while the APCs lined across the farm fields due east could advance on Klein Gastrose with some kind of impunity. He snatched for his radio.

"Chubby! Can you and Brannigan get a shot at those two BTRs on the freeway?"

There was a long pause of crackling static before the radio filled with Chubby Washington's tense voice. He and his loader were dug in just a hundred meters from where the Russian APCs were parked.

"If we open fire this close, we're dead," his voice was a strained stage whisper. "We'll be cut to pieces the moment we launch and expose our position."

"Damn it, if you don't take those two APCs out, we're all going to die," Purcell realized the suicidal implications of his order.

Chubby's voice turned heavy and fatalistic. "Roger that."

The line went dead.

The two Russian APCs opened fire, hammering the hotel and sending a withering fusillade of bullets along the street. The sound was deafening; a maniacal roar of violence, supported by the lighter, less frantic spatter of infantry light arms. The Devils returning fire from the hotel windows had no choice but to throw themselves down to the ground behind whatever cover they could find and ride out the tempest. And with every passing second the Russian BTRs scattered across the plowed fields were closing inexorably.

Purcell flung himself sideways just as a torrent of machine gun fire tore ragged plaster chips from the window frame. Broken shards of glass flew like shrapnel across the room. One of the Devils suffered facial cuts and another cried out, clutching at a deep gash in his arm.

The thundering roar of suppressing fire went on interminably, tearing plaster from the ceiling, shattering furniture and filling the room with debris. Purcell clutched his helmet to his head and tucked himself into a tight ball. He could feel the walls of the hotel vibrate through a series of earthquake-like aftershocks.

The sound of a sudden ear-splitting explosion was appallingly loud and so unexpected that for a moment the battlefield seemed to lapse into shocked eerie silence. The swathe of hammering machine gun fire stopped abruptly, to be replaced by the noise of muffled screams. Purcell crawled back to the window and stole a cautious glance along the freeway.

The closest BTR was on fire, burning fiercely, the tangled twisted ruins of the vehicle scattered across all three lanes of the blacktop. Spot fires had started in the grassy verge of the road and there were dead and writhing Russian bodies lying on the road beneath a wall of black smoke. Purcell stared for another incredulous heartbeat and then flicked his eyes a hundred meters sideways to where Chubby and Scott Brannigan were dug in. He fumbled for his binoculars and the magnified lenses found the men's two bodies, broken and torn apart by enemy machine gun fire. Both men were dead, slaughtered at close range. They lay slumped over their Javelin launcher, eyes open and sightlessly staring up at the sky.

Purcell felt a lump choke in his throat and his eyes prickled with tears. His order had caused the death of both men.

The stunned silence lasted just a few seconds and then the second BTR's heavy machine gun roared into vengeful life, pummeling the hotel and the village buildings nested around the distant intersection. Purcell went to ground again as the fury of enemy fire reached a raging crescendo.

The second Javelin team were still concealed on the opposite side of the road, no more than a hundred and fifty meters from where the remaining BTR was parked. For a perilous moment Purcell considered ordering a second suicidal launch at the Russian APC – then checked himself. He couldn't afford to lose another Javelin team – not while there was still a chance they could hold the Russians off. He reached for his radio and ordered the two men to fall back to the village.

"Get your asses out of there asap," he spoke quickly and urgently.

The second team were dug in north of the road and out of direct enemy fire. They still had a chance to survive the onslaught if they chose their moment carefully.

The team acknowledged the order, and Purcell turned his desperate thoughts to an alternative plan. He needed to destroy the remaining BTR before the enemy personnel carriers approaching through the farm fields reached the outskirts of the village.

G-Spot arrived at the hotel bearing a crate of Molotov cocktails and Purcell eyed the soldier with a grimace. G-Spot was breathing hard, his face tight with fear. He had run the gauntlet of the Russian machine guns to bring the homemade explosives forward and had inadvertently stepped out of the frying pan and into the fire.

"G-Spot, I need you."

"For what?" the man asked innocently.

"I need you to come with me."

"Where?" G-Spot looked about, bewildered. There was nowhere to go. The Russians were tearing the hotel to pieces with a relentless hammering staccato of firepower. The only place to go was to ground: to find cover and ride out the storm.

"We have to take out a BTR two hundred meters down the road."

"Take it out?" G-Spot's face turned pale with dreadful foreboding.

"With Molotov cocktails," Purcell said. "If we don't, every man in the Devil's Detail will be dead within the hour and the Russians will seize the village."

"Jesus Joseph, ever-loving Christ," G-Spot croaked the blasphemy and took an unconscious step backwards. "You're fucking kidding, right?" Twenty years ago, he had served with distinction in Afghanistan fighting the Taliban and al-Qaeda, but nothing in his combat experience had prepared him for a suicidal dash towards an enemy APC. He was the father of two young boys and a husband to his childhood sweetheart, waiting for him back in Pensacola, Florida.

Purcell shook his head. "I wish I was," he said heavily. "But we don't have a choice. This is do or die."

G-Spot steadied himself. He nodded stiffly, because when the chips were down, warriors stood up. "Okay."

Purcell got on comms to Tom Hawker and spoke quickly over the net, his no-nonsense tone putting paid to his XO's vehement protests.

"Keep that Javelin of yours firing until you run out of reloads," Purcell issued his instructions. "Concentrate on the APCs crossing the fields. I'm taking G-Spot forward with me. We're going to try to destroy the APC on the freeway."

"But Frank!" Hawker understood the suicidal desperation of Purcell's plan. "We can hit the fucker with our Javelin."

"Maybe," Purcell grunted. "But we've already wasted one missile trying to do just that from close range. We can't afford to waste another shot. The fucker is hull-down amongst the debris."

"But Frank…!"

"Tom, you're in command. If things start to go badly, bug out in the trucks and save as many civilians as you can. Out."

Purcell cut comms abruptly and slung his M4 over his shoulder. He checked his pocket to be sure he had a Zippo lighter, then snatched up two of the fuel-filled beer bottles from the plastic crate, holding one in each hand.

"Your job is to shoot every fucker we see until we reach the freeway," Purcell got eye-to-eye with G-Spot. Both men were sweating. G-Spot's face suddenly filled with grim, purposeful resolve. "Roger that."

The service door of the hotel opened onto a narrow side alley. The two men loitered in the shadows of the doorway until they heard the enemy machine gun fire taper into a brief lull. Purcell could hear his heart thumping like a drum inside his chest. He nodded once to G-Spot and the two men broke from cover, running crouched along the laneway until it ended abruptly. Purcell peeked around the corner and stared east, stealthy as a thief.

He could see clear to the river, his view lined with tall trees. He crept forward, hugging the rear wall of the hotel until they reached the corner of the building. G-Spot was close behind him; so close that Purcell could smell the other man's fear; a copper-like tang of sweaty desperation, and hear his rasping breath saw across his throat.

At the corner of the building the two men paused again. The Russian machine gun regained its fury, roaring with demonic rage as it renewed its suppressing fire. Purcell sucked in a deep steadying breath, counted silently to three, and then stole a glance beyond the wall.

He could see the freeway, and he could see the Russian BTR. The commander was leaning out of his cupola, hunched behind the machine gun, directing fire straight down the road, oblivious to them. The BTR was wedged nose-first against the burned-out hulk of another APC, using the ruined carcass as cover from anti-tank missile fire. Purcell hesitated. He saw a handful of charred bodies strewn across the blacktop. Those Russians, Purcell guessed, had been killed back when the first APC had been destroyed.

He was about to duck back into cover when a flash of movement caught his eye. He held his position for another heartbeat and saw a squad of Russian infantry lying prone by the verge of the road. They were spread out in the grass, facing away from him and pouring light arms fire into the buildings on the outskirts of the village.

Purcell grimaced. If the infantry were alert and noticed his approach, he and G-Spot would be cut down and killed. He leaned back out of sight and told G-Spot what he had seen.

"The APC is two hundred meters directly ahead, and there are about a dozen infantry in the grass on the south side of the freeway. They're firing on the village. We're going to hook north and take our chances in the long grass on the opposite side of the road. Once we get close enough, I'll hit the BTR with the Molotov cocktails and we'll get out again before the Russian infantry can react to our attack."

It was a desperate plan, but it was the only plan. G-Spot double-checked his weapon and pushed himself ahead of Purcell. He was a solidly-built man, broad across the shoulders and barrel-chested. He had put on twenty pounds since leaving the army and his gut hung heavily over the belt of his pants – but he was still a soldier.

"Stay behind me," G-Spot stirred. "I'll get you there in one piece."

G-Spot went forward, crouched and wary, using the drifting veils of swirling smoke to conceal his movement. Purcell shadowed him, one bottle of fuel in his pocket and the other gripped in his fist. They reached the north side of the freeway and went to ground under the shade of a tree.

G-Spot surveyed the terrain ahead and used the brief interval to catch his breath. He was panting but fighting to control it, and his heart was racing. He could feel clammy sweat break out across the palms of his hands. He got to his knees, then came to his feet, running at an oblique angle to the road, lifting his legs high through the long grass. His dash took him diagonally away from the road and he kept going for a hundred meters before dropping back down into the grass.

He had an unobstructed view back to the road and he paused again to refill his burning lungs. The two men were now sixty meters into the long grassy field and just as far from the freeway, blindside to the Russian BTR. G-Spot pointed.

The Russian APC was broadside to them, partially obscured by steel wreckage. The vehicle's commander was still hunched over his HMG, with his back to them. The Russian infantry were deployed in the grass on the far side of the BTR and were unsighted. It was Purcell's best chance.

"We get closer," G-Spot laid out his plan. "And then I'll cover you while you dash forward and make the attack."

Purcell nodded. He fumbled into his pocket for his Zippo, ready.

G-Spot waited until the Russian APC commander reloaded his machine gun with a fresh belt of ammunition and began firing again. The KPVT-14.5 heavy machine gun was older than even the BTR-50s. The weapon had first entered service in the Soviet army back in the late 1940s but had been withdrawn from production less than twenty years later because it was simply too heavy and too big for the infantry to maneuver effectively. It had been given a fifty-round ammunition belt and mounted on vehicles such as the BTR-50.

As soon as the Russian machine gun opened fire again, G-Spot crawled forward. The smoke drifted in thin curtains about him, like an early winter's mist. He went as close as he dared, then dropped to the ground a final time.

"Thirty meters," he squinted sweat from his eyes and estimated the distance to the BTR. "Are you ready?"

Frank Purcell nodded. He felt like a sprinter on the blocks, about to get the starter's pistol. His legs felt tired, and his breath came in tight little grunts. For the first time in years, he felt like an old man. His knees ached and there was a small tremble in his fingers. Something heavy and slithering turned over in his guts.

"I'm ready," he grunted.

G-Spot settled himself prone in the long grass and took aim at the Russian commander hunched over his machine gun. "If that fucker so much as turns to look at you, I'll put a bullet between his eyes," he vowed.

Purcell took one long final breath and bounded to his feet, running full-pelt towards the Russian BTR-50, the Molotov cocktail in his right hand and the Zippo in his left. He ran straight towards the enemy APC and dropped to his knees in the grass when he was well within throwing distance. He felt breathless and shaky. His shirt was wet with sweat and clinging chill to his back. The roar from the Russian machine gun hammered against his ears and the stench of oil and smoke and diesel overwhelmed his senses. He lit the taper of rag dangling from the neck of the bottle and made sure the flames had caught, then tossed the homemade bomb at the Russian BTR.

The bottle swung through the air in a lazy arc and landed in the troop carrier compartment directly behind the mounted machine gun. Purcell didn't hear the glass smash, but he heard the great 'whoosh' of flames as the fuel caught alight and became an inferno.

The commander leaning out of his cupola turned in astonishment and was consumed by the flames as they washed over the vehicle. The man screamed in shrill pain and clutched at his face, his uniform catching fire and then his hair burning like a torch. He fell from the cupola, writhing in tortured agony as the flames spread across the vehicle, and filled the air with black choking smoke.

Purcell felt a great lift of triumph and relief. He fumbled the second homemade bomb from his pocket and launched it in the direction of the burning BTR. The second Molotov cocktail shattered on the blacktop just short of the burning personnel carrier and spread a fierce wall of flames over the roadway.

"Run!" Purcell heard G-Spot's strained shouting voice through the chaos and the screams. "Fucking run for it!"

Purcell ran.

He jinked back through the grass, exhilarated and gasping and went to ground close to where G-Spot lay. He was too breathless to speak but the two men exchanged triumphant, vengeful smiles.

"Not bad for a couple of old guys," G-Spot grinned, then died.

The Russian infantry on the far side of the burning BTR had reacted to the surprise attack like a swarm of angry wasps driven from their nest, spraying wild fire in every direction, infected with chaos and confusion. A sergeant commanding the men realized the attack had come from the north side of the freeway and hurled himself through the wall of flames. He came through the fire tucked into a tight ball and rolled onto his knees, his assault rifle jammed into his hip and his finger on the trigger. He saw G-Spot raise his head out of the long grass and fired instinctively, hitting the affable American flush in the smiling face. The bullet struck G-Spot in the eye and tore out through the back of his head, sending his helmet spinning in the air and splashing the contents of his skull against Purcell's shoulder.

Frank Purcell gaped, frozen in disbelief and shock – and then a bullet fanned past his face, so close that he felt the heat and the buffeting wind against his cheek. Something demonic and unholy flashed in his eyes. Shock turned to rage. He reached for G-Spot's M4 and got calmly to his feet, firing from the hip at the Russian sergeant, heedless of the danger.

The Russian returned fire, but Purcell cut the man down, his finger tight on the trigger, his mind consumed with vengeance. The Russian died screaming and Purcell kept firing into the corpse until the magazine was empty. Only then did some semblance of sanity return. The rage in his eyes faded and he realized how vulnerable he was. He turned in the grass and ran back towards the village, sobbing his grief and slump-shouldered with guilt.

Chapter 6:

Tom Hawker saw the sudden flash of leaping flames from the corner of his eye and realized instantly what had happened. He leaned closer to the shopfront window where he had his command post and peered down the length of the freeway to where the BTR was burning fiercely.

"Fuck, yeah, Frank!" he whooped in celebration – then turned his attention back to the problem directly ahead of him.

The handful of Russian BTRs spread out across the farm fields east of the village were advancing inexorably behind a curtain of smoke and withering machine gun fire. Hawker guessed the range to be around five hundred meters, but the veil of drifting smoke ahead of the advancing enemy APCs made them ethereal and somehow less menacing so that for long moments he hesitated before finally giving the order to his Javelin team.

"Hit the fuckers!" he growled.

The Javelin team were crouched in the rubble of the shopfront doorway with a clear view east. The loader deftly fitted a new launch tube assembly and clapped the shooter on the shoulder.

"Ready!"

It was close range, and the enemy vehicles were bright stark targets in the CLU's magnified sights. The shooter settled himself in a kneeling position and braced his body for the weapon's kick. He had set the CLU to 'soft launch' to conceal his position from the enemy and to minimize the backblast of the weapon. He took a last settling breath and squeezed the fire trigger.

The Javelin leaped from the CLU, flying low through the haze, wavering slightly as the missile's fins deployed to stabilize its flight. Hawker tried to track the missile with his eyes but lost it in a cloud of smoke. Two seconds after launch the lead Russian BTR-50 suddenly exploded in a great bloom of fire and the sound of the explosion echoed across the sky, drowning out even the drumming chatter of heavy machine gun fire for a moment.

"Hit!" Hawker celebrated and snatched for his binoculars. He could see the burning APC stopped dead in the middle of the field, its demise marked by a rising tower of black smoke. Russian infantry caught up in the blast were scattered dead in the dirt. "Reload!"

The rest of the Russian personnel carriers were still advancing, their heavy steel tracks churning up the soft ground. One of the vehicles slowed to a crawl and the dozen men crouched in the troop compartment suddenly bailed out, tumbling over the side of the vehicle and spreading out across the field. Hawker pointed to get his men's attention.

There were a handful of Devils at the shop's windows, waiting for targets.

"Kill them all. Open fire!" Hawker shouted.

A fusillade of light arms fire swept across the fields, aimed at the Russian troops who had dismounted their vehicle. Two men went to ground with leg wounds almost immediately, but the others threw themselves into the dirt and began to return fire. The commander at the vehicle's heavy machine gun swiveled and fired at the Devils, forcing men to take cover. Windows shattered and bullets punched holes through internal plaster walls the size of a fist. Dust and shards of masonry filled the shop's small front room. Hawker ducked down behind a section of brick wall and felt the heavy *'thwack'* of bullets striking all around him.

The fury lasted for several seconds and then stopped abruptly.

"Fire!" Hawker urged his men in the sudden fraught silence.

The Javelin team had reloaded and were ready to shoot again. The operator locked on to the closest BTR and fired. Another great fountain of fire erupted around an enemy APC as the vehicle was obliterated.

The Russian officer commanding the APCs saw a second vehicle destroyed and lost his nerve. "Fall back! Fall back to the bridge immediately!" he roared across the radio network. To advance any further was to invite certain death. He shouted at his driver to turn back for the bridge and accelerate, then repeated his orders to the surviving vehicles strew across the fields. "Get back over the bridge. Retreat!"

*

General Stavatesky stood beside his BTR-80 command vehicle and watched the debacle from the apex of the bridge glowering and murderous with outrage. He saw the half-dozen remaining APCs turn back towards the bridge in retreat and uttered a tirade of vehement expletives, cursing the son-of-a-whore who commanded the attack, and the useless troops he had been given to carry out his plan.

He turned, still seething, and looked hard at the remainder of his column. He had about twenty more BTR-50s parked in a line, still uncommitted to the fight. For an impulsive, furious moment he considered ordering them forward into the fray – but at the last second icy reason stalled him.

As long as the allies defending the village had anti-tank missiles and men to launch them, he was stalemated. His only options were brutal bloody force... or finesse. He snatched for his radio and snarled.

"Major! Where the fuck are you?"

For a long moment there was nothing but the wavering hiss of static. Stavatesky stood with his fist bunched on his hip, glaring towards the village, stomping his foot with impatience.

"We are across the river and moving north in column," the major commanding the Russian outflanking attack came on the radio, his voice loud over the rattle and roar of his vehicle's ancient diesel engine.

"How long until you reach the village?" Stavatesky barked.

Another brief pause. "Ten minutes. We are five kilometers south of Klein Gastrose."

*

Frank Purcell reached the safety of the hotel, haggard and still burdened with the heavy weight of G-Spot's sudden death. He sagged through the doorway in the sudden lull of the Russian retreat and drank thirstily from a canteen.

The hotel looked like it had taken fire from a battery of enemy artillery. Parts of the ground floor ceiling had collapsed and the plush carpet was littered with masonry dust, plaster and shattered shards of glass. There were hundreds of bullet holes punched through walls, and doors had been shattered. Purcell trudged up the stairs and stood in the hallway for a moment. He could see blood against one wall, and he could hear the moans of wounded men. He followed the sound to the west side of the building. A room had been turned into a temporary aid station. Four men were lying prone on the floor, each of them bloodied and in agony. A fifth man, on one knee attending to one of the wounded, looked up with weary eyes of exhaustion.

"Anyone dead?" Purcell forced himself to ask.

"No," the soldier answered and bent to wrap a leg wound in bandages. "These boys will recover."

Purcell grunted with relief. The Russian attack had failed, and casualties had been minimal. He sighed and felt some of the tension drain from his body. Then his radio crackled to life, and he snatched for it instinctively.

"Purcell."

"Boss, it's Bluey," the voice of the big Australian twanged in Purcell's ear. "I'm three clicks south of your position and in place defending the ridge overlooking the highway. I wanted you to know that we've got a mother-fucking shit-load of trouble heading straight towards us."

*

The fifteen BTR-50s under the command of the Russian infantry major crossed the river well south of Klein Gastrose without incident and formed up on the highway in column, facing north. The major placed his own vehicle fifth in the line and switched his radio to the battalion net to issue his orders.

"We advance at best speed," he said. "When we reach the German village, we do not halt. We attack with guns blazing. Our surprise assault against the enemy's undefended flank must be a shocking hammer blow they cannot recover from. Go! Go! Go!"

The road north was deserted but there was a steady stream of civilian traffic heading south. The vehicles were piled high with furniture and the German civilians in their cars gaped with astonished curiosity when they saw Russian APCs barreling past them in the opposite direction.

The major stood up in the command cupola of his vehicle with his binoculars pressed to his eyes, surveying the terrain ahead. The ground was fertile farmland, lush and green and forested. Neat stone houses sat back from the road behind wooden fences and there were cattle grazing and wildflowers growing along the roadside. It was an idyllic summer's afternoon, eerily tranquil – broken only by the dirty diesel belch of exhausts and the menacing roar of military armor on the move.

The road ran arrow-straight and against the horizon line the major could see the far away smudge of smoke like an angry scar drawn across the sky. He estimated the German village was just a few miles ahead, and he was tempted by caution to slow his advance, but the risk of the General's vindictive ire put that notion swiftly from his mind. Every second mattered.

The freeway was four lanes wide, dipping down into a shallow valley and then beginning to rise, turning slightly as it curved to pass through the shadowed saddle of a rock-strewn ridgeline. The major set down his binoculars and slid down inside the vehicle's internal compartment to issue orders to his driver.

"Keep your speed up," he spoke sternly to the young corporal. "The village is in the valley just beyond that ridge ahead."

He stood back up through the cupola and ordered one of the infantrymen hunched in the troop compartment directly behind him to man the vehicle's heavy machine gun. Beneath his feet he felt the APC's big engine seem to vibrate as the driver accelerated to maintain his speed as the road began to gently climb. Then the major heard one of the soldiers inside the troop compartment suddenly swear in alarm. A blink of an eye later the APC in the vanguard of the advance exploded inside a fireball of roaring flames.

"*Yebat!*" the major swore in utter astonishment as the flaming wreck ahead of him became engulfed in oily smoke. He threw himself down inside the APC and bellowed at his driver. "Get off the fucking road!"

The column of BTRs swerved left and right, spilling off the freeway and blundering into the fields on either side of the road. The major got on the radio and screamed. "Did anyone see the missile launch?"

The destroyed vehicle was a ghastly wreck of twisted metal; the men riding in the troop compartment killed instantly. The major flung his binoculars to his eyes and scanned the ridgeline ahead of him carefully, feeling vulnerable and dreadfully exposed. There was no hard cover for his vehicles to hide behind; nothing but open fields dotted with trees. A few seconds later he caught sight of a flash and then a streak of grey smoke came hurtling towards the convoy.

"Get out of the vehicles!" the major shouted a warning, but his voice was drowned out by revving engines. An APC in the field on the opposite side of the freeway suddenly exploded.

"Fuck!" the major roared. He could hear men screaming and the radio net suddenly jammed with near-hysterical panicked voices. The major shouted into his handset. "Open fire on the fucking ridge line. The enemy are defending the saddle of the road. Open fire and kill the vermin!"

The Russian HMGs had an effective range up to three thousand meters and the pass through the ridge was less than a kilometer away. A dozen machine guns opened fire simultaneously. Two of the BTRs popped smoke to conceal their positions and the battlefield became a place of noise and disorder. Through the chaos the major tried valiantly to marshal his force.

"Keep firing and keep moving. Advance towards the ridge. We must get through that pass and into the valley beyond."

*

"Fire!" Bluey gave the order to his Javelin team when the closest Russian BTR was just a thousand meters away.

He and his handful of men were spread out across the ridge and hidden behind rock outcrops, covering the pass. They had seen the enemy convoy approaching from several kilometers away, but Bluey had deliberately waited until the BTRs were close enough to bring them to the edge of small arms fire.

The missile flew from its launcher and slammed into the lead vehicle in the convoy, obliterating it into a thousand flying pieces of shrapnel. Then the crew reloaded and fired again, striking a second enemy APC. The road south of the pass turned into a place of terror and confusion.

Bluey had hoped the surprise attack would be enough to halt the convoy and force them to fall back, but the Russians had continued to drive doggedly forward in the face of danger, spreading out into the fields on either side of the freeway as they began to pop smoke and counter-fire. Now the Devils were cowering under a withering hail of HMG fire that tore at the ridge line and forced them to seek shelter.

Bluey shouted at his Javelin crew. The team only had two reloads left and their mission was to block the pass.

"Get down the slope and take the LandCruiser," he had to bellow above the incessant hammer of enemy fire. "Drive north towards the village for a kilometer and find a firing position from where you can see the pass. As soon as the Russians reach the saddle of the ridge, open fire with your last couple of reloads and block the road."

The Javelin team slithered back off the crest of the rise and dashed down the slope. The LandCruiser was parked nearby. They roared off in search of a new firing position while Bluey and the three men he still had with him prepared to return fire on the Russians.

Bluey stole a glance at the approaching APCs as enemy bullets plucked and tore at the air around his head. They had closed within five hundred meters of the ridge, the vehicles weaving like drunkards behind a shifting curtain of smoke. As they drew closer to the pass, they began compressing together, merging back towards the blacktop.

"Fire!" Bluey ordered the men operating the M240 machine gun.

The M240 opened fire, not with any clear targets but instead with the intention of causing confusion and panic amongst the enemy soldiers sheltering in the open-topped troop compartments of each APC. They were vulnerable to attack from elevated firing positions and soon bullets were clanging off the armored hulls and getting hits. One rifleman was struck in the head and slumped forward on his bench seat, his face hideously distorted and the back of his skull matted with blood. Another man in the following vehicle screamed in sudden pain and clutched at his shoulder. The Russian infantry returned fire, shooting back as their vehicles jounced and juddered through the plowed fields until the battlefield was a heaving cauldron of wild noise and smoke and horror.

"Keep firing!" Bluey urged the men around him, rising to his knees to shoot down into the maelstrom, firing blindly into the drifting billows of smoke.

The Russians were tenaciously still advancing, and the fire being poured onto the ridgetop increased in volume and venom until the air around the Devils turned thick with dust and death. The gunner behind the M240 was hit in the shoulder by an enemy bullet and the brutal impact almost severed the man's arm from his body, breaking bones and shredding flesh. The man rolled away, white-faced with shock, his eyes monstrous as the pain washed over him in great waves. Then the loader was struck and killed instantly. The Russian heavy machine gun rounds were capable of downing low-flying aircraft and punching through the hull armor of allied IFVs like the Stryker. The damage it did to a man was absolutely cataclysmic. Bluey gaped at the steaming mess of gore that had only a second ago been a friend and felt himself consumed with rage.

Rising to his knees and careless of the danger of the storm swirling all around him, he fired down into the smoke, emptying his M4s magazine, his lips pulled back, his teeth bared in a rictus of savagery. He ducked down behind the rocks just long enough to reload and then rose again, the fury still seething within him, the need for retribution boiling in his blood. He emptied a second magazine into the Russian BTRs then threw himself down behind cover, gasping and panting for breath as the Russians returned fire.

The enemy APCs had forced their way to within a few hundred meters of the pass and now began to form up on the road, heavy machine guns still firing. The vehicle in the vanguard reached the pass, accelerating as it pushed through the breach – and then exploded in the middle of the blacktop; killed by a Javelin missile.

Bluey heard the thunderclap of the explosion and cheered. He flung a couple of grenades down onto the road, not even bothering to wait for the explosions before he rose again to a crouch and continued firing.

The BTR that was second in line swerved around the ruins of the lead vehicle and was also hit flush by a Javelin missile, effectively blocking the pass with a wall of flames and a tangle of mangled wreckage. Bluey let out a ragged cry of triumph – and then was flung backwards by the almighty punch of a Russian HMG round that struck him in the thigh, amputating his leg below the knee.

He fell back, gasping and panting, staring up at the sky as the pain assailed him. He could feel himself dying; feel himself bleeding out as his blood pumped from his horrendous wound into the dirt. He blinked away sweat from his eyes and gasped on a choking breath, then fumbled the radio from his belt.

"Outpost South to Devils Six actual," he croaked.

In the village hotel, Frank Purcell responded immediately with a sense of sick foreboding. It was the first time he had ever heard the Australian soldier use something resembling official military comms protocol.

"Bluey. SITREP!"

"The pass is blocked," Bluey gritted his teeth and gasped the words, his face wrenched into a grimace of stabbing pain. "I reckon we've bought you fifteen or twenty minutes until the road can be cleared. There's still about ten Russian APCs to deal with."

"Roger that," Purcell grunted. "Get back to the village asap."

"I can't do that," Bluey's voice turned almost regretful. "Requesting permission to die like a boss instead," his voice sounded wretched with agony and Purcell suddenly realized the Australian must be badly wounded.

"Denied!" Purcell shouted into the radio handset as a choke of emotion caught in the colonel's throat. He pictured the big Australian peppered with bullet wounds of cut to pieces from shrapnel. "Denied, soldier! You get your ass back here. That's an order!"

There were a few gasping seconds of labored breathing and then Bluey transmitted for the final time. "Sorry, Frank. Have a beer with the boys to remember me."

*

When Purcell raised Tom Hawker on the company net, he was still distraught with grief, his tone almost fatalistic with resignation.

"Tom, Bluey's dead, and I think the other men with him are as well," Purcell relayed the radio message from the Australian. "He said the pass to the south of us is temporarily blocked but there are still about ten BTR-50s that will be bearing down on us in fifteen minutes. What's your Javelin reload SITREP?"

"Bluey's dead?" Hawker reacted with the same sudden dismay.

"Yes. Chubby Washington and Scott Brannigan have bought it too. So has Skinner and Sullivan, and I've got another five who are seriously wounded."

"Shit."

"Yeah."

Hawker took a moment to gather his frayed thoughts. "My team only has two Javelin reloads left," he said. "And I've got three dead and six wounded. Baker took a hit to the chest. He might not survive."

Purcell grunted. "My Javelin team has one reload left."

Hawker did the math and knew the numbers didn't add up. "Frank three reloads between us isn't enough. The enemy must have at least another twenty BTRs on the Polish side of the bridge and ten more closing in on us from the south."

"I know."

"And we're down to maybe eighty men."

"I know."

"What do you want to do?"

Purcell held the radio to his mouth and stared off into empty space for a long moment as if hypnotized by the billowing black clouds of smoke that stretched across the skyline. The battlefield seemed eerily silent in the aftermath of the recent firefight. He made his decision.

"I'm abandoning my position," the colonel decided. "We're going to contract back along the freeway to your location and join what's left of our forces together. We have to concede these outskirt buildings to the enemy and make our last stand at the intersection."

*

1st Platoon vacated their positions from the buildings around the hotel and fell back along the freeway towards the main intersection, carrying their wounded with them and using the drifting smoke to conceal their retreat.

Purcell was the last man to leave, standing sentry duty in one of the second story hotel windows, watching the distance for signs of an enemy attack. He had thought long and hard about the hopelessness of their situation. If he was the Russian commander, this was the time he would advance; surging his APCs over the bridge at the same moment the column of BTRs to the south began to close of Klein Gastrose. Attacked from two directions simultaneously, the Devils would be unable to hold out for more than a few frantic minutes before being slaughtered.

When the last of the wounded had been carried out onto the street, Purcell took one last long look towards the bridge and then dashed down the stairs and out onto the sidewalk.

None of the Devils were running; they were falling back in an orderly fashion. But when they reached the buildings that 2nd and 3rd Platoon were doggedly defending, a sudden explosion made Purcell turn in alarm. He saw a fountain of dirt rising from the edge of one of the plowed farm fields and then a few seconds later another explosion landed just short of the hotel, tearing a hole in the sidewalk concrete and throwing up a shower of shrapnel and debris.

"Mortars!" Purcell turned and barked at his men. "Get your asses under cover, pronto!"

The Devils dashed into the buildings around the intersection and Purcell found Tom Hawker standing by a café window that afforded a tree-filtered view all the way to the bridge.

"82's?" Purcell took a wild guess. He was panting, breathless and sweating. His face was caked in streaks of grime.

"Yeah, looks like it," Hawker said darkly as a third mortar round landed in the middle of the freeway, directly across from the hotel. "They're finding their range. The Russians must have set up a mortar battery on the far side of the river. It can only mean they're getting ready to launch another attack."

The two officers exchanged meaningful glances. Once the enemy had zeroed in on the intersection, there was going to be hell to pay and nothing the Devils could do except hunker down in cover and pray to their god for mercy.

"Is everyone in good cover?" Purcell snatched a glance at the bullet ravaged walls around him.

"Good enough to survive machine gun fire," Hawker qualified. "But against mortars?" he shrugged. "Where is safe?"

There were six Russian 82-BM-37 mortars arranged atop a small grassy knoll about five hundred yards east of the river, being operated by the dismounted infantry and personally supervised by General Stavatesky. They were ancient weapons, first introduced into the Soviet army back in the late 1930s and still in service. Rugged, reliable and functional, each mortar was capable of hurling munitions three thousand meters; more than enough to reach the tiny German village on the far side of the river.

"Keep firing you idiots!" Stavatesky had his binoculars pressed to his eyes, watching the fall of each ranging shot. "You're still dropping short. Fix it!"

The mortar crews worked with exaggerated care, adjusting the elevation of their weapons and firing consecutively until a round finally landed on the intersection, blowing a hole in the blacktop. Stavatesky allowed himself a grunt of satisfaction.

"Now pound the scum until every building is destroyed and every one of the enemy are dead," he said.

*

Frank Purcell and Tom Hawker sat hunched under the cover of a dining table, their backs against a wall, as the Russian mortars began to fall from the sky and wreak havoc on the tiny village. A round fell short and struck the hotel, exploding a hole in the roof that brought down a section of the eastern façade. Dust and debris filled the air and fire broke out. The next enemy mortar round flew long and landed in one of the narrow village side-streets, ripping up pavement cobblestones and shattering the windows of a butcher shop.

Purcell glanced at his watch.

"Any minute now the column of APCs approaching from the south are going to come into range. Is everything prepared?"

Hawker nodded bleakly. The survivors of 1st Platoon had joined the men of 2nd Platoon in the buildings south of the intersection where they expected the next attack to come from. The Canadians, French, British and Polish recruits that made up 3rd Platoon were defending the buildings to the north.

"The two Javelin teams and our last three reloads are in position defending the road from the south," Hawker said. "They have orders to open fire as soon as they see the column approaching. The men are ready. They know what's coming."

Purcell grunted and cocked a listening ear for the fall of incoming mortars. He heard a distant explosion and saw a flash of fiery light from somewhere a few hundred yards to the east and figured one of the buildings close to the hotel had taken a hit. The sound of the explosion echoed along the street and then was drowned out by another explosion, much closer.

"Stay here and keep an eye on the bridge. If the Russians have any brains at all – and no one ever accused them of being stupid – they'll use this mortar fire to screen another attack."

"Where are you going?" Hawker looked perplexed.

"The trucks," Purcell said. "We've got one last chance to get the remaining Devereaum people and the civilians out of harm's way. If we don't send them west now, we might not get another opportunity."

He waited for a temporary lull in mortar fire and dashed through a rear door into one of the narrow alleys, wending his way through the village's side streets to where the remaining MAN KAT-1s were parked. The milling crowd of civilians and Devereaum people cowering in the open street were near frantic with alarm, groaning and flinching every time an enemy mortar exploded close by. Only the handful of armed Devils stationed to supervise the loading were restraining the masses from anarchy.

"Get on board!" Purcell saw just three of the heavy trucks remaining, parked in a line. "Get on board!" he shouted into the pale fraught faces. Gary Wrexford, Devereaum operations manager, was amongst the throng and Purcell singled he man out and seized him roughly by the arm. "Get everyone onto a truck, now!" he snapped. "The trucks are moving out."

Panic erupted. An incoherent roar of fear rose from the press of bodies and people began to clamber towards the trucks, using shoulders and elbows to fend others off. Someone shouted and a punch was thrown. A man fell into the gutter bleeding from the nose. Purcell drew his sidearm and fired one shot into the afternoon sky. The crowd froze, fear etched deep into their faces.

"Act like men, not fucking rats!" he glared at the throng, his lip curled into a snarl of disdain.

The moment each truck was filled to cattle-like capacity, Purcell gave the driver instructions and the vehicles went roaring away, lumbering under their swaying loads of desperate humanity until all three trucks had departed and the sidewalk and street were deserted.

Purcell felt a rush of relief and a prickle of regret. He had done his job; his mission had been accomplished – but the cost would be the lives of every one of the Devils. Now, there was no means of escape. The Devil's Detail would be forced to fight to the death.

When he returned to the building where Tom Hawker waited, Purcell was downcast and resigned. He slumped down alongside the tall black officer and mopped sweat from his brow with his fingers.

"It's done?" Hawker asked.

"Yes."

"Now we really are fucked."

"Yes."

There seemed nothing more to say and for a long moment the two men sat and stared bleakly out through the smoke haze towards the distant bridge.

"You were right, Tom," Purcell admitted after an awkward pause, his voice seeming to ghost out of the gloom like the haunted moan of a spirit. "We *are* too old for this shit," he smiled wryly when he saw the surprise of Hawker's face and rushed to qualify. "It's not the fighting," he shook his head. "That's intuitive to both of us. That training and instinct cannot be eradicated – not even by the passage of time. But it's the emotional toll we're too old for. It's the loss of friends, the burden of responsibility, the consequences of a man's death on his family, his loved ones, his children… I'm too old to shrug those tragedies off. When I was regular army, it was just an ugly truth of combat. Death happened, no matter how hard you tried to protect your men. But now? Now it hurts more. Death has more weight because as an old man with a wife and kids of my own, I finally understand the ramifications; the gravity of loss. The older I get, the more I hate the pure futility of war."

Tom Hawker sat, stony-faced and contemplative. At another time and in another place, Purcell's quiet and insightful wisdom might have moved him to tears. He grimaced, and then suddenly an idea came to him; vague and ethereal at first, like a whisp of breeze. He closed his eyes and hunted his mind for the elusive flash of inspiration but it remained shady as smoke, lurking in the shadows of his consciousness. Then a Russian mortar round landed in the street just outside the building, tearing at the shopfront wall and throwing up a curtain of dust and debris. The sudden shock seemed to jolt the idea loose and suddenly it was there, right in front of him, fully realized and promising hope. He turned to Purcell, his eyes glittering with excitement, and seized the other man's arm.

"Frank! I think I have a solution. But I need one of the LandCruisers and I need sixty minutes."

"What?" Purcell looked incredulous.

"Can you hold this place for an hour?"

It was a moment that didn't require any tactical appraisal or an assessment of threats. All it demanded of Purcell was unwavering trust in a man who was a soldier and his friend.

"Yes. We can hold."

*

Purcell watched Tom Hawker throw himself behind the wheel of the LandCruiser and tear off at high speed in an urgent snarl of tire smoke and dust. Hawker raced northwest on the same road that had brought the Devils to Klein Gastrose.

Fourteen minutes later the Russians attacked.

Chapter 7:

"Frank!" RTO, Pat Devline, raised Purcell on his handheld radio. "You better get your ass to the south side of the village, boss. The fucking Russians are coming."

Purcell ran at full-pelt through the side streets and burst through a back door into a coffee shop on the southern outskirts of the settlement. He swarmed through the building until he found a window and peered hard into the distance.

South of Klein Gastrose the road to Forst ran through a shallow valley in a series of gentle turns, passing through lush farm fields filled with grazing cows. A neat cemetery stood atop a gentle rise, with sweeping views east to the river. Purcell took in the lay of the land instantly and clenched his jaw tight. Russian BTRs were advancing in a column along the road, drifting in and out of sight behind clumps of trees and dilapidated farm sheds. He guessed they were about two kilometers away, but closing steadily. He studied the vehicles through the lens of his binoculars, then turned and glanced about him.

Pat Devline was in the shop's stock room, still desperately trying to raise help from the Big Army, shouting his frustration into his radio gear and hissing threats to anyone who responded to his calls. Around him were four other men, including a two-man Javelin team. They were standing at a waist-high wall beside an archway that opened onto an outdoor client dining area, scattered with wooden tables and chairs, and strung with decorative lights.

Purcell crossed to the Javelin team. There was a single reload for the anti-tank weapon lying on the ground at their feet.

"Are you locked and loaded?" he asked.

The two men were tense and grim-faced. The operator tore his eyes away from the CLU screen just long enough to give a curt reply.

"Yeah."

Purcell nodded. "Then fire."

There was no point in waiting until the Russians closed, Purcell figured. The road could not be obstructed, and it was simply an inevitable matter of time before the enemy closed and the chaos of close combat ensued. Better to hit the enemy at long range and give them some reason for uncertainty. The Javelin was deadly accurate up to two thousand meters.

The operator had the CLU already set to the system's default 'top attack' mode. He took a long moment to double-check the settings and then squeezed the trigger. The missile leapt from its tube, kicking up a backblast of flame and dust and flew high into the darkening afternoon sky.

Purcell tracked the launch but soon lost the missile in the drifting veils of smoke that lay like a shroud across the village. He zeroed his binoculars onto the Russian column and waited impatiently, his heart beginning to trip with tension. Four seconds after launch the second BTR in the Russian column blew apart and was consumed by a mushroom cloud of flames and smoke. It took a full second before the echo of the explosion reached Purcell's ears. By that time the APC was already burning fiercely.

The sudden and unexpected explosion caused immediate panic amongst the Russians. The surviving troop transports spilled off the road and into the surrounding fields, battering through farm fences to search for shallow folds in the ground that might afford them cover. Purcell watched the pandemonium. He turned to the Javelin crew with a grim reaper's smile.

"Hit them again," he said.

The crew had one last missile left. They went through the reload process with deliberate practiced moves while Purcell kept his glasses fixed on the Russian BTRs. Some of the enemy vehicles had stopped in the fields, but a few heroic drivers were still pushing forward, sticking to the road and accelerating. Purcell watched the range close inexorably, fighting against his impatience until the Javelin team had power to their unit and were once more ready to fire. The operator squeezed the seeker trigger and set the target gate over the BTR in the vanguard of the column, aiming at the center of the vehicle and then boxing it in on all sides with the fiddly adjustment controls to ensure the thermal signature from the enemy APC was clearly identified by the CLU's computer. He waited to be certain the vehicle had been acquired by the system and then braced himself as he squeezed the fire trigger.

The Javelin launched from its tube and went arrowing skywards before beginning its terminal attack. The target BTR-50 was picking up speed along a section of straight road, pulling ahead of the rest of the convoy, when the missile struck suddenly from above. The Russian troop carrier blew outwards like it had been crushed by an artillery round, the massive impact cartwheeling dead bodies into the sky and shredding the vehicle's steel hull into tiny pieces of shrapnel. For a second the wreckage was obscured by flames, and then black smoke began to boil into the sky. The vehicles following the APC veered back off the road in chaotic confusion and ground to a halt by the gravel verge of the blacktop.

Purcell watched the attack and then set down his binoculars. "That's going to cause the enemy some consternation," he said aloud to the two-man crew. "The Russians don't know whether we've got more Javelins or not, so they're going to hesitate until someone in command reorganizes them and renews the advance. Use the time you have left to dig in; find anything you can for cover and keep low. Make sure you have a handful of Molotov cocktails ready. The next time the enemy attack, petrol bombs will be our only way of stopping them."

He went out through the door grim faced and burdened with worries. He had a single Javelin reload left and he went to find the crew. He discovered them in the ruins of a clothes store that had been heavily damaged by Russian HMG fire. The building stood close to the intersection with views east to the bridge and south to the outskirts of the hamlet.

The two-man crew were concealed in the rubble near the front door, kneeling behind a section of low brick wall. They saw Purcell appear from the rear of the building, then ducked suddenly and clamped their helmets to their heads as an enemy mortar round landed in the street outside. Shards of stone and shrapnel pinged and fizzed through the air. Purcell waited for the aftershock of the explosion to pass, then crawled forward and crouched down close to the Javelin crew. He noticed their weapon was loaded and ready for firing.

"That's our last Javelin," Purcell said pointedly. "We can't afford to waste the shot and you can't afford to miss your target, so don't fire, under any circumstances, unless I give the order. Understand?"

The operator nodded. His face was caked in grey dust and streaked through with runnels of dried blood from a head wound. His eyes were bloodshot with exhaustion and fatigue, his face tight with fear. He jerked his head to acknowledge the order then shot a nervous glance sideways at his loader before speaking.

"We're not gonna make it through this, are we colonel?"

Purcell flinched. "There's always hope," he said.

"The trucks are gone. I saw them leave. There's no way out of this village now except in a body bag."

"There's always a chance," Purcell said stoically. "Sniper's Nightmare is still on comms trying to arrange reinforcements, and we've hit the Russians pretty darn hard. They can't keep attacking forever," he put confident steel into his voice and kept his face expressionless, lest the man see through the flimsy of his lie. "All we've got to do is hold tight and keep fighting."

An enemy mortar round landed in the street outside the building, and then another landed flush on the hotel a few hundred yards away, collapsing one wall of the building and spilling rubble across the blacktop. It seemed to Purcell that the intensity of the barrage and the tempo of enemy fire had suddenly accelerated – an ominous prelude to an imminent attack. He left the Javelin crew and wended his way northwards through the debris, moving from building to building, passing on orders and instructions to the Devils as he moved. When he reached the ruins of a pharmacy the mortar bombardment suddenly stopped. Purcell glanced at his watch, then towards the east. Through the smoke and haze he could suddenly see enemy APCs on the move, crossing the bridge to launch yet another attack.

He felt his shoulders slump with despondency. "We've run out of time," he muttered bitterly to himself.

Because the Russians were attacking from the east and from the south – and the Devil's Detail had no weapons left to fight them with.

*

The Russian APCs swarmed over the bridge and began to scatter off the freeway as they approached the ravaged outskirts of Klein Gastrose. The lead troop carrier braked to a halt in front of the ruined hotel and the soldiers sitting hunched on their benches suddenly spilled over the sides of the vehicle. They went to ground on the blacktop, scavenging for cover amongst the debris while the HMG aboard the APC covered their disembarkation.

The rest of the convoy braked just long enough to allow the troops they were carrying the opportunity to clamber over the sides, and then pushed on, the drivers quickly crunching up through the gears to gather speed.

The first tanks had appeared on a modern battlefield over a hundred years earlier at the battle of Cambrai, and ever since that time one rule of warfare had remained constant; *armor never fought in an urban environment without close infantry support.*

The Russians were experts at urban warfare. The men commanding their armies were the sons of Stalingrad's heroes, and so the Russian infantry dispersed across the fields and prepared to advance into the face of enemy fire as the APCs trundled forward.

General Stavatesky watched the attack go in from the crest of the bridge, standing close to his command vehicle. He sighed visibly with relief when the first BTRs reached the outskirts of the hamlet without taking enemy fire. It was enough to give him hope, and he leaned in through the door of the BTR-80 and bellowed at his radio operator.

"Find out where the rest of our APCs are! The attack from the south must be launched now!"

The radio operator raised the infantry major on the battalion net and hunched over his gear for a long tense moment. He acknowledged the response and turned to Stavatesky, red-faced and sweating. "The major says he is a kilometer from the village and advancing at full speed."

"Good. Acknowledge," the General allowed himself a moment of grim satisfaction. Finally, his plan was coming to fruition. The afternoon had been fraught with setbacks and unexpected challenges but now, at last, his military genius would be revealed. He turned back smugly towards the battlefield and pressed his binoculars to his eyes.

The outskirts of the hamlet were eerily quiet and the APCs were forming themselves into a line across the farm fields, unmolested by enemy fire. Around the steel beasts swarmed the infantry, moving in a ragged straggle but nonetheless moving forward. Then, in the far distance, he heard a rattling throaty roar of machine gun fire hammer the air. It was the signal he had been waiting for.

The attack from the south was driving forward.

Stavatesky leaned back through the open door of his command vehicle. "Get the mortar crews on the line. Tell them to stop firing immediately."

The time for preparation and maneuvering was over. Now it was time to close on the enemy and kill them all.

*

"Wait!" Frank Purcell shouted the warning, so his words carried amongst the rubble of the building. "Wait for my order," he stared fixedly out through the shattered glass of the shopfront's window at the advancing enemy. The Russian APCs were moving purposefully, drifting in and out of shifting smoke, grey silhouettes against a darkening sky.

Purcell could feel the nervous tension ratcheting up as the Devils prepared to fight for their lives. They were all sweating and exhausted, many carrying wounds. They hunched behind cover, hearts thumping. Some men mouthed silent prayers to their god. Some recited verses from the bible. One man reached into his pocket for a faded polaroid of his wife and kissed the grainy image a last poignant farewell.

Some Devils thought about their families; their children and their elderly parents while others checked and re-checked their weapons with compulsive repetition.

Then a roar of machine gun fire cut through the charged tension, sounding far away and obscured. The radio on Purcell's hip crackled, then erupted in desperate frantic shouts.

"Colonel! The fucking Russians are hitting us from the south. They're about half a click from our position and closing fast!" the voice sounded frayed and on the edge of hysteria.

The waiting was over.

"Fire!"

The Javelin team armed with the last remaining reload already had a Russian APC locked on and in their sights, the CLU set to 'direct attack'. The range was less than four hundred meters. The operator squeezed the fire trigger, and the missile flashed from the tube and went rocketing straight towards its target. The BTR blew apart and the echo of the explosion shook the air with a thunderclap of violent noise.

The surviving Russian APCs surging across the farm fields immediately responded with a fury of vengeful HMG fire, blazing away at the buildings around the intersection and forcing the Devils to cringe behind cover as the tempest of heavy rounds disintegrated furniture and punched fist-sized holes in the walls. A man went down screaming, bowled over backwards by the elephantine impact of a hit to the chest. He was dead before his body hit the floor. A nearby Devil scampered impulsively from cover to render the victim aid and was also killed, his body gruesomely mangled by the frightening killing power of a Russian High Explosive Incendiary - Tracer (HEI-T) round.

"Jesus!" a Devil who had witnessed the dreadful carnage sobbed aloud and blinked away tears of raw terror. "Jesus wept! They're both fucking gone, man. They're both dead. They look like they've been savaged by lions."

"Fire!" Purcell shouted again and despite the suicidal danger, the Devils manfully forced themselves from cover and began shooting at the Russian infantry. Bullets sparked off the steel hulls of the BTRs and cut a swathe through the enemy's troops. Two Russian riflemen running beside an APC and using the vehicle's bulk for shelter were cut down, both hit in the legs. They fell screaming to the ground and were crushed beneath the tracks of a trailing BTR as it swerved around rubble.

"Fire!" Purcell aimed his M4 at a soldier wearing an officer's uniform. The man had his hand raised, waving a pistol in the air and screaming orders to the troops clustered about him. Purcell's bullet caught the Russian in the side of the head and bowled him over. Purcell continued firing, emptying his magazine into the smoke, and then reloaded in a few brief seconds of deft, practiced movements. He fired again at an enemy rifleman running across the blacktop but missed.

"Fire!"

One of the M240s in a building at the northern end of the intersection roared, catching a handful of enemy soldiers in a withering crossfire. Seven Russians went down in the hailstorm. Three were killed outright. One soldier was hit in the stomach and fell writhing in agony. Another had both his legs shot out from underneath him and fell on the blacktop, twisted with excruciating pain. The APC that the enemy troops had been using to shelter their advance turned its machine gun onto the building where the Devils had shot from and all-but demolished the stone and wood façade with a relentless fury of counter-fire. The two Canadians from 3rd Platoon who had been hunched behind the M240 were both killed, and a Frenchman defending the far corner of the building was grievously wounded. Purcell watched the violence unfold and gritted his teeth at the helpless futility of their situation.

The company net became a chaos of shouted messages, each one garbled and made incoherent by the hammering noise of combat and the rising panic in the voices.

"We need more fucking ammo. More ammo for fuck's sake!"

"Christ! Jackson just bought it. He's guts are splashed across the fucking wall."

"I need backup here. Backup goddamnit, now!"

"Jimmy is down! Repeat, Jimmy is down. He's bleeding out. Where's a fucking medic?"

Radio comms between the Devils had always been informal and now, caught in the eye of the storm and fighting for their lives, the PMC was suffering because of it. Purcell snatched at his handset and had to shout to be heard.

"Clear the fucking net!" he roared, venting his temper. "All Devils get off this fucking line unless you have tactical comms to transmit!"

The radio chatter died but the sound of battle rose to a crescendo. The Russian BTR-50s on the southern outskirts of the village suddenly reached the outlying buildings, traveling at top speed to run the gauntlet of allied fire. With their machine guns targeting every shopfront that lined their route to suppress enemy resistance, they barrelled along the freeway towards the intersection.

The column rumbled past the ruins of a small grocery store and then a real estate office, a soldier standing behind the HMG of the lead vehicle swiveling the weapon from side to side as each building passed by. A Devil crouched in the rubble of the real estate office lit a Molotov cocktail and flung the bomb, unsighted, out into the street. It landed on the tarmac in front of the convoy and exploded, spreading leaping flames across the road. The first Russian vehicle blew through the wall of flames and emerged on the far side of the inferno blackened and scorched. The trailing APCs all slowed, and in that brief moment of opportunity two more Devils bravely emerged from the smoke, homemade bombs in hand. The first beer bottle filled with fuel struck the side of a passing BTR and exploded, painting the vehicle's hull in burning fuel. The driver of the vehicle panicked and screamed, then crashed the APC into the wall of a shop. The second Molotov cocktail arced through the air, spinning end-over-end in flight, before landing inside the open troop compartment of the following vehicle. The bomb exploded amongst the seated infantry, causing carnage. A tower of black smoke hid the ghastly moment, but nothing could conceal the piercing shrill screams of the Russian troops as they were incinerated. A blackened figure fell onto the road, the man's clothes on fire, his hair burning like a torch. His eyelids and lips had been scorched from his face and his flesh was livid red as it burned. He thrashed on the ground, drumming his heels, a high wheezing sound of unimaginable agony in his throat, until the flames overwhelmed him.

The rest of the column slewed to a halt in the middle of the freeway, hemmed in on both sides by bullet-ravaged buildings and their route forward to the intersection suddenly blocked by a wall of flame. The enemy infantry penned inside their troop compartments added their small arms fire to the heavy thunder of the HMGs as panic rose amongst the Russians.

Into that flaming chaos, more Molotov cocktails fell.

One landed on the rear engine compartment of a stalled APC and burst into flames, engulfing the vehicle in smoke, but most of the bombs the Devils threw fell short of their targets and exploded on the sidewalk or the street. The Russian infantry had no choice but to abandon the safety of their vehicles. They spilled over the sides and went to ground on the blacktop, firing wildly into the buildings around them.

"Advance!" the infantry major joined his men on the road, trying desperately to restore order. His troops were white-faced with confusion and anxiety, cringing away from the flames as they flashed and flared all around them. The major understood that this moment was critical. If the Russians could attack immediately, the enemy defending the buildings would be overwhelmed and quickly killed. But if the Russians delayed moving forward, the battle could turn into a dangerous stalemate. He turned and glowered at his troops.

A Devil hidden in the ruins of a delicatessen lobbed a hand grenade out onto the sidewalk and the explosion roared like a clap of thunder. It caused no injuries to the enemy, but added to their rising panic.

"Advance on the buildings!" the major roared again, gesturing angrily with his arms to urge his men forward. Close quarters combat in an urban environment was typically loathed by infantry who despised the harrowing nerve-wracking danger, and the Russians troops were reluctant to dash forward into a new savage hell. Most of them blatantly ignored the order and continued firing into the buildings from the relative safety of the far side of the road.

"Advance!" the major stood red-faced with humiliation and outrage, ignoring the spatter of bullets that plucked at the air around him. He glared at his troops, his face twisted with an expression of monstrous betrayal and kicked a nearby rifleman in the guts. "Move, fuck you! Move!" he vented his outrage by swinging his boot at another man cowered behind the hull of an APC. He seized the rifleman manfully by the collar, dragging him out into the open. "I said attack!"

The major pushed the man hard in the back and the rifleman stumbled forward. He was immediately cut down by shrapnel from an exploding grenade. He fell on his back screaming in pain, his uniform shredded and his face a mask of blood.

More Molotov cocktails landed on the street, bursting into flames and the Russian infantry shrank away. The major pushed another man towards the inferno, threatening the rifleman with his own weapon. "Attack!" he bellowed, then turned his fury on a knot of soldiers who were all firing from behind the hull of an APC. "All of you will advance and –"

A sudden spray of bullets caught the major in the chest and knocked him backwards. He fell bleeding to the blacktop on his back, his eyes wide with astonishment and dismay. His mind had just a fleeting second to register the fact that he had been murdered by one of his own mutinying men before he died.

With the infantry major killed, the Russian infantry attack south of the village lost momentum and the battle devolved into a grim standoff with the Devils holding their ground and the Russians unwilling to advance and unable to quickly withdraw. Both sides continued to exchange gunfire but it was clear that the Russians had no desire to force the battle into a house-to-house street fight. Slowly the infantry began to contract away from the firefight, leaving their APCs isolated and without close support.

Pat Devline got on comms to Purcell, the RTO's voice breathless with urgency.

"We're holding the southern outskirts," he shouted into the radio. "The Russian column has been stalled and we're beating them back."

"Casualties?"

"Some," Devline conceded. "But the Russians are taking a hammering. I think we can fight them off – at least for the moment."

Purcell acknowledged the message, though it was small relief because the main force of enemy APCs that had crossed the bridge were still closing remorselessly on the intersection and here the Russians were fighting smart. Keeping their BTRs out of close weapons range, their vehicles had been parked hull-down behind rubble at intervals along the street from where they could lay down covering fire, safe in the knowledge they were well out of Molotov cocktail range. Under that blanket of relentless heavy weapons cover, the Russian infantry were remorselessly working their way forward, advancing in short darting bursts from building to building, working in small groups as they fired and moved, fired and moved again.

Purcell couldn't help but be grudgingly impressed. If he had been commanding the enemy troops, he would have attacked the exact same way. He stood back from his vantage point for a heartbeat, knowing the inevitable was almost upon him.

The Devils were still fighting bravely, popping up from cover to fire short bursts at enemy targets, and then ducking back into safety as counter-fire cracked and fizzed about them.

But it could only be a matter of time before the first enemy troops gathered themselves to storm the buildings and the battle devolved into the terror-stricken chaos of a close-quarters nightmare.

One of the Devils in the same room as Purcell rose bravely from cover and threw a grenade out into the street then fell backwards in agony, struck in the shoulder by a salvo of enemy small arms fire. The man staggered back against a wall and then sagged slowly to the floor, clutching at his wound, blood seeping between his fingers. He was a grey-haired veteran from North Dakota who had fought during Desert Storm. He choked on a wave of pain, then gritted his teeth, spitting blood.

"I'm alright. I'm alright," he grunted, then fell dead to the ground.

Another of the Devils inadvertently ducked into a fusillade of light machine gun fire and was killed as he sought better cover. He fell headlong through a splintered doorway and didn't move again.

In frantic desperation, several of the Devils began lobbing their fire bombs out onto the street, throwing up a wall of flames and smoke between themselves and the enemy. The leaping inferno forced the enemy infantry to reel away and the black oily smoke temporarily obscured the buildings from the enemy's HMGs, giving the beleaguered Devils a small respite. The village intersection became a fiery cauldron and for several minutes the battle seemed to sink into an ominous lull.

During that brooding hiatus Purcell considered the ignominy of surrendering – and then dismissed the notion; not out of pride, but out of practicality. The Russians were in an evil mood. They had been humiliatingly repulsed three times and suffered serious losses. They would want violent revenge, not prisoners.

"Keep firing!" Purcell reloaded his M4 and fired into the flames as more Molotov cocktails were hurled onto the street. "Don't let the bastards reach the buildings. Cut them down! Cut them down!"

There was nothing else to do. The Devils could only die fighting.

Chapter 8:

Tom Hawker drove northwest like a man possessed, flinging the LandCruiser across the road, weaving in and out of the traffic stream like he was driving a pursuit car in a high-speed police chase. Civilian vehicles loaded with furniture and towing trailers were fleeing towards safety, choking the road, but Hawker overtook them all, veering onto the wrong side of the blacktop and ducking back into traffic only at the last second to avoid accidents.

He drove with his foot pressing the gas pedal to the floor, sitting hunched over the steering wheel and snarling at each small delay. He pounded the horn and growled with frustration, his face tight and wrenched with desperation. He overtook a family sedan, then ducked back into the traffic flow in the face of an oncoming truck. Then he passed a stream of cars by hurtling along the gravel shoulder, the LandCruiser slewing and fishtailing precariously on the loose surface.

"Move your ass!" he yelled at an SUV with suitcases stacked atop the roof racks.

The LandCruiser's engine bellowed and the vehicle leaped forward, swerving back onto the wrong side of the road. Hawker peered anxiously through the windshield, then flicked a glance at his wristwatch.

"Faster! Faster!"

He reached the turnoff to the LRRP and swerved off the road without slowing. The Landcruiser's big tyres screeched in protest and then the vehicle was bucking across plowed fields like it was out of control. Inside the cabin, Hawker was flung about like a boat on a storm-tossed ocean. His teeth slammed painfully together, and the taste of blood flooded his mouth. He steered for a cluster of tents in the middle of the grassy paddock, his foot never touching the brakes until he reached his destination. The Landcruiser swung violently in a muddy skid and heaved to a sickening halt, almost shooting the tall black officer through the windshield before stopping.

Hawker was out from behind the wheel and running before the engine died. A group of soldiers came towards him, two carrying M4s, alarmed by the threat of the speeding vehicle. Hawker searched the faces of the soldiers and recognized the lieutenant who had given them fuel for their trucks.

"Lieutenant Dunn," Hawker was breathless and his hands were trembling, adrenalin fizzing in his blood. His face dripped sweat and his uniform was torn and stank of smoke. Hawker doubled over, propped his hands on his knees and forced himself to draw three deep settling breaths before he straightened again.

"Lieutenant Dunn, The Devils PMC urgently need your help."

"The Devils?" the young Lieutenant looked bewildered.

"You gave us petrol earlier today for our MAN KAT-1 trucks."

A light of recognition went on behind the young officer's eyes and he nodded, then turned solemn. "What kind of help?"

"Our mission was to rescue civilians from the village of Klein Gastrose, close to the Polish border. But the Russians have attacked. Forty or fifty APCs crossed the river earlier this afternoon and have mounted an assault on the settlement. We managed to evacuate the civilian population, but the company are pinned down and in danger of being overrun."

Lieutenant Dunn looked incredulous. "You can't be serious," for a moment he figured this was some kind of elaborate practical joke. "Everyone knows the fighting is taking place north of here."

"I'm deadly fucking serious!" Tom Hawker's temper flared. "My buddies are fighting and dying right now. They're outnumbered against Russian armor! We're throwing fucking Molotov cocktails for Christ's sake because we've got nothing else left to fight them with."

"If this was true, I would have heard something," Dunn hesitated, then said with wary caution.

"We've tried radioing for help but no one in the Big Army will listen to us because we're just a PMC," Hawker blurted in a few short sentences. "But this shit is real, lieutenant, and if something isn't done right now, then the Russians will seize the village and will try to turn the allied southern flank. The fight for Germany could be lost. If the enemy can capture the village and get a column of tanks into our rear..."

Still Dunn remained unconvinced. He scrutinized Tom Hawker's face for any trace of deception or mockery.

"Assuming what you're saying is true," the young lieutenant shifted his feet uncertainly, "what the hell do you expect us to do? We're just an LRRP."

"I want you to get on the blower to anyone and everyone and alert the army to the threat. We need fighter support. We need reinforcements before it's too late. And I need one of those M1A1 tanks you're servicing," he turned and pointed across the field to where the three Abrams were parked beneath a grove of trees.

"You're kidding."

"Do I look like I'm fucking joking?" Hawker took a menacing step forward, his face ugly and brutal with emotion.

"I can't authorize –"

"You don't have to," Hawker cut the lieutenant off. "I'm taking one of those tanks. Now you can either shoot me or help me."

Dunn hesitated. The two men stood toe-to-toe, one still aged in his twenties, fresh faced and filled with the arrogance of youth, and the other middle-aged and worn down by life's struggles. One was bound by an army's rules and regulations and the other was appealing for the lives of his friend and brothers-in-arms.

Dunn nodded, then grimaced. He would almost certainly lose his commission over his decision. "Okay," he conceded.

"And I need men," Hawker insisted. "Someone who can drive, someone who can work the gun, and someone to load."

For a moment Dunn's face reacted with a flinch of dismay, and then he nodded again. "Jenkins and Clover are trained on the M1," he volunteered the two mechanics that Hawker had met earlier in the day. "They can drive and fire the weapon. I'll be your loader."

"You?" Hawker blinked. "Have you served in an M1?"

"No," the Lieutenant shook his head, "but if I'm going to get court-martialled for this crazy stunt, I'm damn-well going to be a part of the action."

*

The most battle-ready Abrams at the LRRP was the one in the middle of the line. The vehicle was fully repaired and almost ready for return to its unit. Jenkins and Clover were in the process of reloading the tank's ammunition rack when Hawker and Lieutenant Dunn appeared, running towards them.

"Fire up the engine!" Hawker shouted as he ran. "What's our loadout situation?"

The two mechanics turned towards the sudden shouts, looking bewildered. Lieutenant Dunn reached the M1 carrying CVC (Combat Vehicle Crewman) helmets and quickly explained.

"This tank is going to war, and we're going with it," Dunn growled and threw a CVC helmet at each of the mechanics. "Jenkins, you're driving. Clover, congratulations. You're now a gunner."

Hawker clambered up onto the M1's hull and stood for a moment. "What's our loadout?" he asked the critical question again. Jenkins and Clover had been in the process of re-loading the tank's ammunition now that all the repairs had been completed. Clover spoke first.

"There are ten rounds of HEAT (high-explosive anti-tank) and another ten of sabot in the rear bustle storage compartment on the 'ready side'. We haven't finished the reload."

"It will have to do," Hawker made the snap decision. "We don't have any time to waste. Jenkins, get down into the driver's compartment and get the engines running. Pronto."

"Where are we going?" Jenkins paused, bewildered and struggling to take on board all this sudden information.

"We're going to war, boy," Hawker said. "We're going to kick some Russian butt."

Jenkins wriggled down through the driver's hatch on the top front of the hull and slid into the driver's station. He reclined back in the padded seat. He pulled the hatch closed behind him and fiddled with the adjustable periscopes until he had a clear view ahead of the tank. Settled in his seat he thumbed the Abrams' engine start button. A heartbeat later the great engine turbines began to spool up, the wine growing steadily. Jenkins flicked a glance at his display screen and saw the display read 'engine start in progress' and the RPM counter begin to rise. He watched the fuel gauge flicker and then the screen settled, glowing green in the confines of the dark hull.

The three other men clambered down through the turret hatch. The heart of the tank was the fighting compartment built within the turret basket. Hawker squeezed into the TC (tank commander's) position at the upper right rear of the turret. Clover wriggled past him into the gunner's seat, ahead of Hawker and lower down inside the turret to the right of the main gun. Lieutenant Dunn stood to the left of the main gun and looked awkward and disorientated. Hawker pulled on his CVC helmet and Dunn did the same, giving all four men internal comms. They needed close communication to be heard above the whine of the turbines.

For Hawker, it was like coming home after being away for twenty years. The sights, the smells of sweat and oil, and the gutsy rumble of the vehicle through the steel hull were like fond reminiscences of the prime of his life. He drew a deep breath, and despite the urgent drama of the moment, he smiled.

"Hello, my love," He muttered.

Jenkins reached for the motorcycle-style handlebar and gave the tank full throttle. The huge gas turbine engine roared. Tom Hawker's voice came through the speakers in the CVC helmet.

"Let's go!" his voice crackled.

The Abrams rumbled forward, gouging deep furrows in the soft grassy field. It reached the highway, and Jenkins turned the tank towards Klein Gastrose.

"Full speed." Hawker insisted.

The Abrams leaped forward and quickly accelerated, trailing a great plume of dust in its wake, barreling down the freeway at almost sixty kilometers an hour. The stream of civilian traffic fleeing in the opposite direction saw the great tank approaching and veered to the gravel side of the road until the Abrams blew past.

As they raced towards the village, Hawker gave Lieutenant Dunn a crash course in loading the Abrams' M256 120mm smoothbore cannon, instructing him from the commander's seat.

They went through the procedure twenty times, rehearsing the loading steps until Dunn had the movements memorized. Hawker judged the lieutenant lamentably slow, but that wouldn't matter, he figured. Unless the Russians had moved a column of T-90s across the bridge in his absence...

"Do it again!" Hawker growled because perfect practice made for perfection. "And keep doing it until you can complete the process in less than five seconds."

The door to the ammo rack slid open and Dunn pulled out a round of HEAT, taking its uncomfortable weight in both hands and holding it to his chest like an infant. He pivoted on his heels, turning the munition as he moved and pushed the round into the breech, then closed it.

"Ready!" he said.

"Too slow," Hawker complained. In truth, it took several weeks of practice to complete the demanding procedure in just a few fluid seconds. "And when you've completed the loading and the gun is ready to fire, you say 'up!', not 'ready'."

Dunn repeated the process again. And again, until his arms ached and he was lathered in sweat. He could feel his lungs burning in the suffocating warmth of the tank's interior and his fingers felt numb. The miles sped by until Hawker could see a dark cloud of smoke on the horizon, and he felt himself tense.

"Klein Gastrose in the distance," he spoke the warning. "We're about six clicks away. Everyone get ready for a shitstorm."

The road dipped down the slope of a hill into a shallow valley of farm fields, then flattened out. Hawker ordered Dunn to load a round of HEAT.

"We're doing this for real now," he warned gravely. "So don't fuck it up. And the moment the breech is closed, back yourself up against the wall so you don't get killed by the recoil when we fire. Understand?"

It was a new, deadly complication for the lieutenant to deal with. He nodded his head, then went through the loading process yet again, setting a HEAT round into the breech and preparing the weapon for firing.

"Up!" he said, then pressed himself back to keep clear of the big gun's wicked kick.

With the Abrams loaded and ready for battle, Hawker turned his attention to tactical considerations. He needed to get into the fight as quickly as possible, and he knew that Russian BTR-50s alone were no threat to an MBT like an Abrams. What he didn't know was whether the Russian mechanized infantry were equipped with anti-tank missile weapons.

"Fuck it!" he decided and snarled. He'd have to take the risk. He needed to swoop on the Russians like wolf amongst a flock of sheep, not stand off passively and hit the enemy from long range. Surprise was everything in battle and the best sudden attacks were swift, lethal and delivered from close range.

The distance between the Abrams and the village closed quickly and with each passing second more details of devastation were revealed. Black smoke hung like a cloud in the air, struck through with leaping flickers of firelight. Then the rooftops of the buildings came into sight. Some of the outlying structures had been reduced to rubble. Others were smoldering and on the verge of collapse. Hawker felt his guts tighten with apprehension and for a long moment he peered ahead with a sinking feeling of despair because he feared he was too late. Then an explosion shook the air followed by a flare of flame and the snarling chatter of machine gun fire, carried on the fluky breeze.

Hawker's spirits lifted and his mood turned vengeful with wrath.

The road to the intersection ran arrow straight for the last two kilometers and for the first time Hawker and his makeshift tank crew had a view of the battlefield, stretching east to the bridge. Ruined Russian BTRs were littered across the landscape but closer to the village all they could see was a chaotic swarm of steel hulls and smoke. To Hawker it seemed like the battle was reaching its climax; the Russians had reached the village center and were fighting for the intersection, pouring machine gun fire into the surrounding buildings.

Hawker checked the range on his commander's screen, measured by the laser rangefinder.

Fifteen hundred yards.

He made his decision.

"Gunner, HEAT, stationary PC."

"Identified!" Clover said after an interminable pause. He laid the muzzle's boresight mark onto the target as he worked the rangefinder and waited for the Abrams' ballistic computer to provide the fire control system with an accurate firing solution. As an afterthought he remembered to engage the tank's stabilizing system. "Identified and acquired!"

The fire control computer did the rest of the work, adjusting the aiming point to account for wind, air temperature, barrel droop and a handful of other obscure factors that might affect accuracy, then began updating its computations thirty times every second.

Hawker let out the tight breath he had been holding. Clover might have been familiar with the tank's computer control systems, but he certainly wasn't battle-ready competent. The process of acquisition had taken what seemed like a lifetime. He set his frustration aside.

With a round already loaded, there was nothing more to be done. Hawker watched the village come closer through his command periscope then gave the order.

"Fire!"

"On the way!" Clover thumbed the trigger on his controls.

The Abrams was charging ahead at high speed, dipping and swaying as it closed on the village. The round flashed from the muzzle and the tank's sophisticated stabilization system kept the barrel steady as a surgeon's hand. The HEAT round reached the snarl of BTR-50s clustered about the intersection in the blink of an eye as the big gun's recoil rocked the tank on its suspension.

The nearest Russian APC suddenly disappeared behind a booming thunder-like roar and a fierce flaming explosion. The Abrams' punching power was cataclysmic. The APC was vaporized instantaneously into a million tiny steel fragments.

"Hit!" Clover cried triumphantly.

"Reload!" Hawker barked at Lieutenant Dunn.

The sudden unexpected explosion caused pandemonium around the intersection. For a moment the battlefield seemed to flinch in shocked dismay. Then the Russians realized an Abrams MBT was bearing down on them. Confusion turned to chaos and then utter white-knuckled terror.

One of the BTRs turned its HMG onto the approaching Abrams and rounds pinged off the tank's armor, causing no damage. All that moment of belligerent defiance did was identify the BTR as a target.

Hawker narrowed his eyes and gave the order.

"Gunner, HEAT, stationary firing PC. Hit the fucker!"

"Identified!" Clover went work, clumsy and flustered under pressure, finally acquiring the target and locking the range into the computer.

"Dunn? Are we loaded?" Hawker had to prompt the lieutenant.

"Almost," Dunn too sounded like a man under intense pressure. "Up! Up!" he cried, then threw himself back and away from the breech.

"Fire!" Hawker growled.

The range was less than a thousand yards, the Abrams storming towards the village like an enraged bull shown a matador's red cape.

"On the way!" Clover pressed the trigger, and the big gun fired again.

The flash flared from the muzzle and a split-second later the mighty boom of the gun echoed on the air. At the same instant the Russian APC blew apart, engulfed in smoke and flames. The killing power of the HEAT round was absolute, punching the personnel carrier backwards across the blacktop and tearing the hull wide open. Every man within twenty feet was killed in the horrific aftermath of the blast, leaving just a charred mangled chassis and the sweet sickly stench of burning flesh. For a moment the village was obscured by oily black smoke.

The Abrams charged on, dust billowing in its wake. Inside the fighting compartment the air had turned thick and stifling and reeked of fumes. Clover and Dunn were dripping sweat from their exertions in the claustrophobic confines. Only Hawker seemed detached and clinical. For him, this was a homecoming. He was back where he belonged.

The veil of smoke cleared from the village to reveal the surviving Russian BTRs hastily reversing back along the freeway, fleeing east towards the bridge and the border. Hawker had no intention of letting the enemy escape unmolested. He was in a dark pitiless mood.

"Gunner, HEAT. Reversing PC close to the intersection!" Hawker noticed the enemy troop carrier and gave Clover the details. The vehicle was backing away, the BTR's commander still firing his HMG into the shopfronts the Devils were dourly defending. As the APC began to withdraw, a knot of Russian troops fell back from the buildings, using the vehicle's steel hull for shelter.

"Identified!" Clover began to warm to his work, quickly acquiring the target.

"Up!" Lieutenant Dunn shouted a few seconds later.

"Fire!" Hawker ordered.

"On the way!" Clover unleashed fresh hell.

The Abrams rocked back on its suspension as the big gun boomed and the breech slammed back. Tendrils of gas and fumes wafted through the turret and a veil of dust drifted on the air.

The impact of the HEAT round blew straight through the Russian BTR, knocking the fourteen-tonne vehicle onto its side like it was a Hollywood prop. The round exploded amidst the Russian vehicle's engine compartment and ignited the fuel tanks. The vehicle went up in a great 'whoosh' of flames, incinerating a dozen enemy infantrymen. The dead lay strewn across the blacktop, eviscerated by shrapnel, their clothes ablaze and their bodies hideously disfigured.

"Jenkins, take us forward, fast," Hawker insisted.

"Roger that," Jenkins acknowledged the order, and the Abrams seemed to find another gear. The tank reached the outskirts of the village and broke through the cauldron of carnage like it was running a blockade, shunting mangled wreckage and rubble out of its way, crushing dead Russian bodies beneath the steel tracks. The tank jounced and swayed and the four men inside the great steel beast were flung about. Dunn staggered violently, cracked his shoulder against the gun's breech, and reeled away with his face wrenched in agony.

"Are you alright?" Hawker spoke quickly on comms to the lieutenant.

"I'm okay," Dunn lied and gritted his teeth. His arm was numb from the elbow joint to the wrist, his fingers seized like a claw.

"Can you reload?"

Dunn said nothing. He drew another HEAT round from the storage rack but could not take the bulky weight of the munition. Clover slid from the gunner's seat and took over the loading. Dunn slumped down, his arm like a broken wing clutched across his chest.

"Reloaded," Clover thrust the round into the breech.

"Jenkins!" Hawker thought fast. The Abrams had reached the intersection and to the east, the enemy BTRs were reversing towards the bridge. To the south Hawker could see nothing but a wall of flames stretched like a bright orange curtain across the blacktop. "Stop! Stop! Stop!"

Jenkins stomped on the brakes and the Abrams lurched to a halt. Clover squeezed himself back into his seat. Hawker peered through the commander's viewing ports and set his attention on a BTR five hundred meters to the east. The vehicle was turning on its tracks, popping smoke and about to engage its forward gears. Hawker could see Russian infantry in the troop compartment, still firing their weapons towards the village buildings. Bullets clanged off the Abrams hull and a spatter of grenade fragments rattled against the turret, sounding like a fistful of gravel thrown against a window.

"Gunner, PC, five hundred meters east, popping smoke and turning," Hawker described the target.

Clover took three ragged heartbeats before he responded. "Identified!" he cried, confirming range with the laser rangefinder.

"Fire!"

"On the way!" the leap of the gun seemed more pronounced now that the Abrams was stationary. The sound of the shot was like the crack of a whip as the breech slammed back despite the built-in ear protection of the CVC helmets.

The round flew down range in the blink of an eye and even before Clover had finished shouting the words in his mouth the BTR blew apart in a gruesome fireworks display of flames and smoke. Through the viewing ports, Hawker watched the impact with a kind of savage melancholy; satisfied that death had been dealt but lamenting the inevitability. The Russian infantry firing from over the sides of the hull never had a chance. They disappeared amidst the flames, engulfed in a blinding apocalyptic instant.

The BTR blew off its tracks, the hull wrenched apart as the round exploded. Huge chunks of burning steel were thrown cartwheeling into the air and plummeted back to the ground.

"Reload!" Hawker hissed, then turned the turret, seeking another target.

Clover slid back out of his seat and went through the laborious process of reloading the gun. By the time a new HEAT round was in the breech, the retreating BTRs had reached the end of the freeway and were fleeing back across the bridge into occupied Poland. Hawker cursed the delay, seething with impatience. The swift execution of violence was a paramount part of a tanker's trade, and having Clover move back and forth from his station to keep loading the gun was costing the Abrams fighting time. His option was to press the injured lieutenant Dunn into the gunner's seat and have Clover load while he took over firing the main gun himself using the commander's override. But by the time he implemented the changes the enemy would have fled across the river to safety.

"Up!" Clover clambered back into the gunner's seat, panting like a man who had run a half-marathon.

"Gunner, stationary command PC on the crest of the bridge," Hawker figured he had time for just one more shot. All he could do was to make it count.

"Identified!" Clover saw the BTR-80 with three whip aerials parked on the bridge and set the laser rangefinder. The vehicle was just under a thousand yards away. The computer crunched the numbers, factoring in all the variables in an instant, and calculated the firing solution.

"Fire!" Hawker barked the order.

Clover sucked in a last gasp of breath and thumbed the fire button. A second later the big Abrams gun roared one final time.

Standing beside his command vehicle and watching the attack, General Stavatesky saw the flash of the Abrams gun and had just a fleeting moment to realize that death was inbound before his command vehicle blew to pieces, killing him instantly in the explosion and firestorm.

*

The Abrams lurched to a halt on the outskirts of Klein Gastrose, slewed across the freeway and facing the bridge. Hawker ordered Jenkins to kill the great engine, and the battlefield turned suddenly silent.

The dust settled and the echo of fighting faded into the darkening sky.

One by one, the crew emerged from the tank, standing atop the hull blinking and shaken by their ordeal. Lieutenant Dunn was helped up through the turret hatch and slumped, breathing hard and his face etched with pain. Tom Hawker leaned against the turret and drew a deep breath.

Slowly the Devils emerged from the rubble-strewn ruins of the buildings, their faces grey with dust, their bodies dragging with fatigue. Most of them were wounded; some superficially, but others would bear the scars of their stoic defiance for the rest of their lives. They stood amidst the debris of the village bewildered and astonished they had endured hell and survived.

Frank Purcell emerged from the shadowed ruins of a restaurant, limping from a bullet wound to his leg and bleeding. He met Tom Hawker in the middle of the freeway and clapped his XO on the shoulder.

"You saved us," Purcell said.

Hawker modestly side-stepped the praise. "I had help," he turned to acknowledge his makeshift tank crew.

Someone amongst the Devils raises his voice into a ragged cheer of relief and others joined in the celebration. A RAF Typhoon FGR4 fighter jet flashed low over the village, appearing from the west and then banking hard, giving rise to bitter grumbles from the Devils that, as always, the bloody Air Force was too late to the fight.

Purcell put his arm around Hawker's shoulder and led his XO a short distance from the others.

"You said you were too old for this shit, Tom," Purcell reminded Hawker through a gentle smile.

"Yeah," Hawker grinned ruefully. "I guess I was wrong. It's nice to know that despite all the grey hair and wrinkles of middle age, the soldier's instinct remains."

They turned together and peered back at the haggard faces of the heroes who had survived the bloody fight. Someone just arrived to the battlefield would have seen a ragged collection of old men, exhausted and sagging, past their prime. But Hawker and Purcell knew better. They saw the Devils for who they really were.

They were brothers-in-arms. They were veterans. They were ageless warriors.

And they had beaten the god-damned Russian Army against all odds.

RUSSIAN FORWARD COMMAND POST
TWO MILES EAST OF GORZYCA,
POLAND-GERMANY BORDER

Epilogue:
Three days later.

The three men entered the Russian command bunker unannounced and stood in the threshold for a menacing moment, silhouetted against the outside light. They were hard-faced figures dressed in long black leather coats.

The senior officer glared about the dugout until his dark eyes caught sight of Chief of the General Staff Army General Mikhail Timoshyn, hunched over a map table, his big bear-shaped bulk somehow withered and rumpled by the hard weeks of fighting.

"Timoshyn!" the senior officer snapped arrogantly. "Cease all activity immediately and come with us."

On the far side of the bunker, the General straightened slowly, and his eyes turned flinty. He recognized the men instantly; not their faces, but their haughty conceit. They were *zampolit*; Russian Army Political Officers.

"Who the fuck are you to speak to me this way?" the General's growled defiance.

"I speak on behalf of the President of Russia," the *zampolit* officer self-assuredly stood his ground. "You are summonsed to Moscow. We have a helicopter waiting."

"I am too busy," Timoshyn dismissed the demand with a glib swat of his hand. "I'm trying to win a fucking war, you fool."

The *zampolit* officer flinched like he had been slapped in the face and for a moment the force of his gaze wavered. Then he steeled himself. "The President demands your obedience. Come with us, immediately."

Timoshyn hesitated for another long moment, then realized the futility of belligerence. He gave a great theatrical sigh to vent his annoyance and reached for his jacket. The three *zampolit* escorted him from the bunker and stood together outside on a patch of muddy ground.

"Where is the helicopter?" Timoshyn scowled.

"There isn't one," the senior Political Officer drew a pistol from within the folds of his coat. "You're not going to Moscow. Instead, you are to be shot for gross military incompetence, unbefitting a senior officer of the Russian Army. Your summary execution has been ordered by the President himself."

General Timoshyn felt the cold steel barrel against the base of his skull and a split-second later a single shot echoed across the grey sullen sky.

NEWS ALERT:

Nick Ryan is now creating short World War III combat movies!

Check out the 'Nick Ryan's WW3 Films' Patreon page for information about the military action movie currently in production and how you can support the project.

patreon.com/NickRyanWW3Films

Links to other titles in the collection:
- Charge to Battle
- Enemy in Sight
- Viper Mission
- Fort Suicide
- The Killing Ground
- Search and Destroy
- Airborne Assault
- Defiant to the Death
- A Time for Heroes
- Oath of Honor
- The Devil's Detail

Website: https://www.worldwar3timeline.com

Author's note:

For the sake of the story, I have taken the liberty of moving the small German settlement of Klein Gastrose a kilometer north of its actual location and set it on an intersection. I hope readers will forgive this small piece of fiction.

Acknowledgements:

The greatest thrill of writing, for me, is the opportunity to research the subject matter and to work with military, political and historical experts from around the world. I had a lot of help researching this book from the following groups and people. I am forever grateful for their willing enthusiasm and cooperation. Any remaining technical errors are mine.

Jill Blasy:

Jill has the editorial eye of an eagle! I trust Jill to read every manuscript, picking up typographical errors, missing commas, and for her general 'sense' of the book. Jill has been a great friend and a valuable part of my team for several years.

Jan Wade:

Jan is my Personal Assistant and an indispensable part of my team. She is a thoughtful, thorough, professional and persistent pleasure to work with. Chances are, if you're reading this book, it's due to Jan's engaging marketing and promotional efforts.

Dale Simpson:

Dale is a retired Special Forces operator who has been helping me with the military aspects of my writing since I first put pen to paper. He is my first point of contact for military technical advice. Over the years that he has been saving me from stupid mistakes we've become firm friends. The authenticity of the action and combat sequences in this novel are due to Dale's diligence and willing cooperation.

Dion Walker Sr:

Sergeant First Class (Retired) Dion Walker Sr, served 21 proud years in the US Army with deployments during Operation Desert Shield/Storm, Operation Intrinsic Action and Operation Iraqi Freedom. For 17 years he was a tanker in several Armor Battalions and Cavalry Squadrons before spending 4 years as an MGS (Stryker Mobile Gun System) Platoon Sergeant in a Stryker Infantry Company.

Bob Ziccardi:

Captain Bob Ziccardi (Retired) served for twenty-three years in the US Army with twenty-one years on Parachute status, including nine years in the 82nd Airborne. He also served two years in an Armored Battalion in Germany during the height of the Cold War. During his time in the military, Bob deployed to Grenada, fought in Operation Desert Shield, and also served in Northern Iraq, Somalia and Bosnia.